PRAISE FOR
THE CHRONICLES OF STANLEY THE PUG

"Enchanting, and such a sweet tale, woven with apt descriptions of how pugs are so much a part of our lives. Love the book and its darling illustrations. I have a degree in illustration and specialized in painting dogs, freelance, so I really appreciate these darling images of pugs and how they are always present in our lives."

—**Laura Libner**, Loralar Pugs

"*The Chronicles of Stanley the Pug* takes readers on an emotional, educational, and heartwarming journey through the loyalty and unconditional love that only a pug can provide."

—**Frankie Colamarino**, Pugs.co

"In Charles Newhall's beautifully illustrated narrative we journey into the symbiotic relationship of Stanley and his family. Everyone should be so blessed to live with Stanley."

—**Constance Payne**, Professor Emeritus,
constancepaynestudio.com

The Chronicles of Stanley the Pug

by Charles W. Newhall, III

Illustrated by Embla Granqvist

Published by

◤ köehlerbooks™

3705 Shore Drive
Virginia Beach, VA 23455
800-435-4811
www.koehlerbooks.com

The *Chronicles of*
Stanley *the* Pug

1991 - 2008

BY CHARLES W. NEWHALL, III

ILLUSTRATED BY EMBLA GRANQVIST

TABLE OF CONTENTS

INTRODUCTION

This book is dedicated to all pugs, but in particular to Stanley the Newhall pug, generation one, Milton and Gracie Pug, generation two, and Marcus Aurelius Pugumus Maximus, generation three and a new member of the family. It is also dedicated to their cousins, AJ and Bennett, who are members of my son Ashton and his wife Becky's family.

Before pugs, we had German shepherds and Siamese cats. They were wonderful animals, but when pugs joined our family, we forgot all other animals. You see, Stanley told us all pugs have a purpose and the purpose is to help all human beings through the vicissitudes of life. Stanley was a descendant of a long line of honorable and very important pugs, and he carried with him the wisdom accumulated over the ages. All our pugs have taught us crucial life lessons.

I call pugs *short travelers* because they have such short life spans. But without those short travelers, our human lives would have lacked much of the joy, love, and meaning on our long voyages (life spans), all of which we found in the company of our pugs, our canine family.

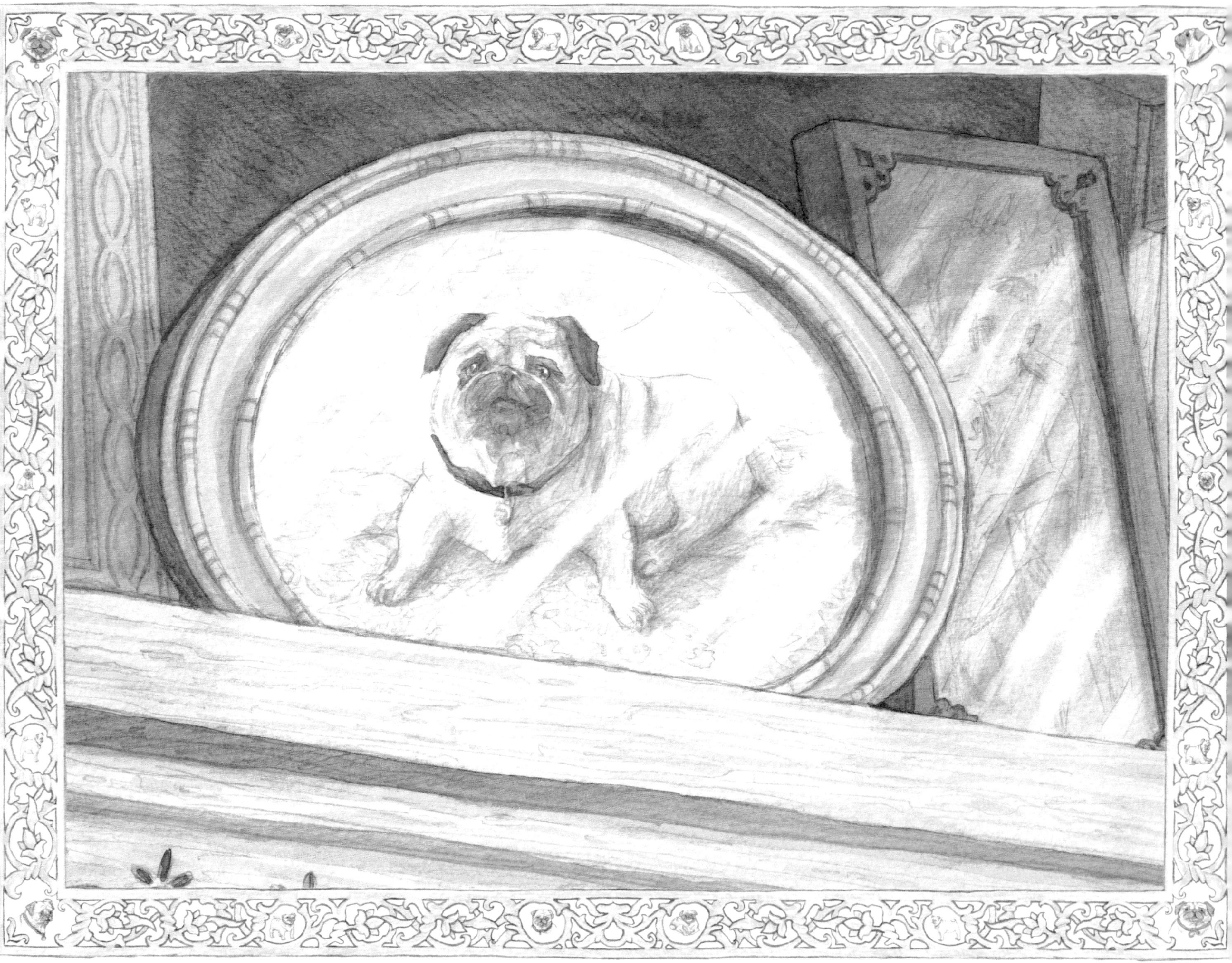

CHAPTER I
A PUG HAS A PURPOSE

My name is Stanley the Pug, and I have a purpose. My purpose is to look after my human family, guide them through the vicissitudes of life, and see that they come to no harm. This has been the task of pugs for thousands of years. We do not choose our purpose; the purpose chooses us. Mine was given to me by my great ancestor, General Celestial Wisdom, and by the emperors of China, but most of all it was given to me by God. If I am not allowed to pursue my purpose, I will shrink into a fur cue ball—useless to all.

Pugs have been bred for thousands of years to know their purpose. Perhaps that is why we are the luckiest of breeds. We are not like the Chihuahuas or the toy poodles whose only purpose is to yap.

Shame on me because *The Way of Pug* says no pug may make mean remarks about other breeds. My only excuse is that I have been living around humans too long.

The Way of Pug was written by my famous ancestor, Lao Tzu Pug, companion of philosopher Lao Tzu. I must apologize because I love to talk about my ancestors. I am not bragging though. I always teach my humans, "If you don't know where you come from, you will never know where you are going." I digress, but that is my weakness. Many pugs have ADHD; our minds jump from one great thought to another.

On the cover of this book, I am shown sitting on a feather pillow and a soft blanket with fringe. Do not be fooled. I am neither feathery nor soft. Like my ancestor the General, I am a philosopher, a warrior, and a scholar. It is just that I find quietude and peace sitting on my pillow. It helps me to think and develop guidance for my humans to help them get through the hard knocks of life. I tell humans to make your life a work of art.

Find tranquility in your beautiful home. Find peace amid fragrant flowers that you grow in your garden. Always live surrounded by beautiful art. These things help you navigate through the tumultuous arena of life.

CHAPTER II
MY ORIGINS

Pugs were the dogs of the emperors of China along with our furry cousins, the shih tzu and Lhasa apso. Empresses of China used to carry us in the sleeves of their robes.

But that was not always the case. We were once a breed similar to bull mastiffs, the giant warrior dogs of China, that fought as soldiers of emperors. Long ago in the Shang Dynasty (1600 BC), an emperor's life was saved in battle by my warrior ancestor named Ferocious. Ferocious led a campaign against the Northern Barbarians. After the battle, Ferocious won the confidence of his enemies and instituted a peace that would last for centuries. Many centuries later, the Northern Barbarians would conquer the Empire of China, led by Genghis Kahn. The Ming emperors who ran China at that time had no

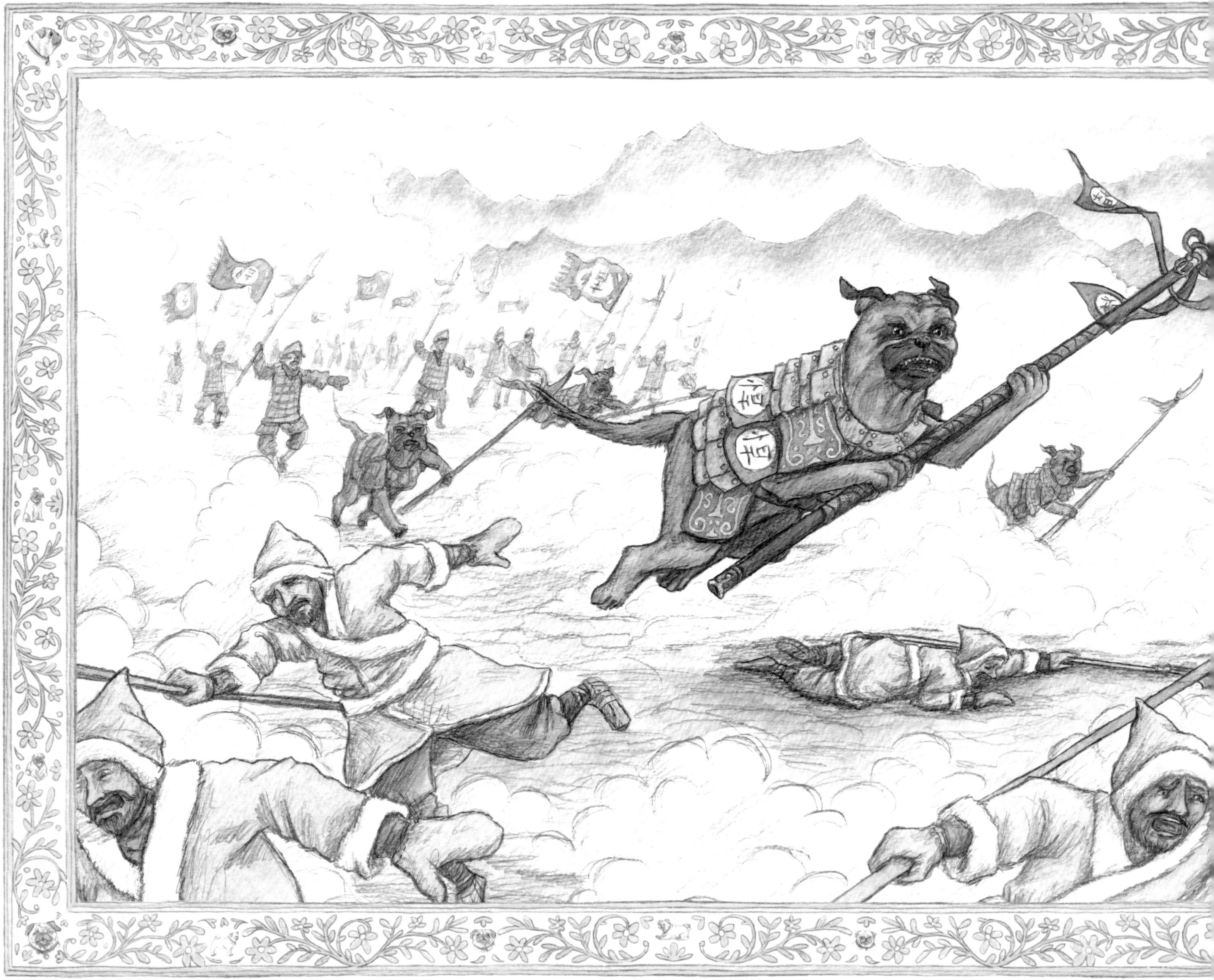

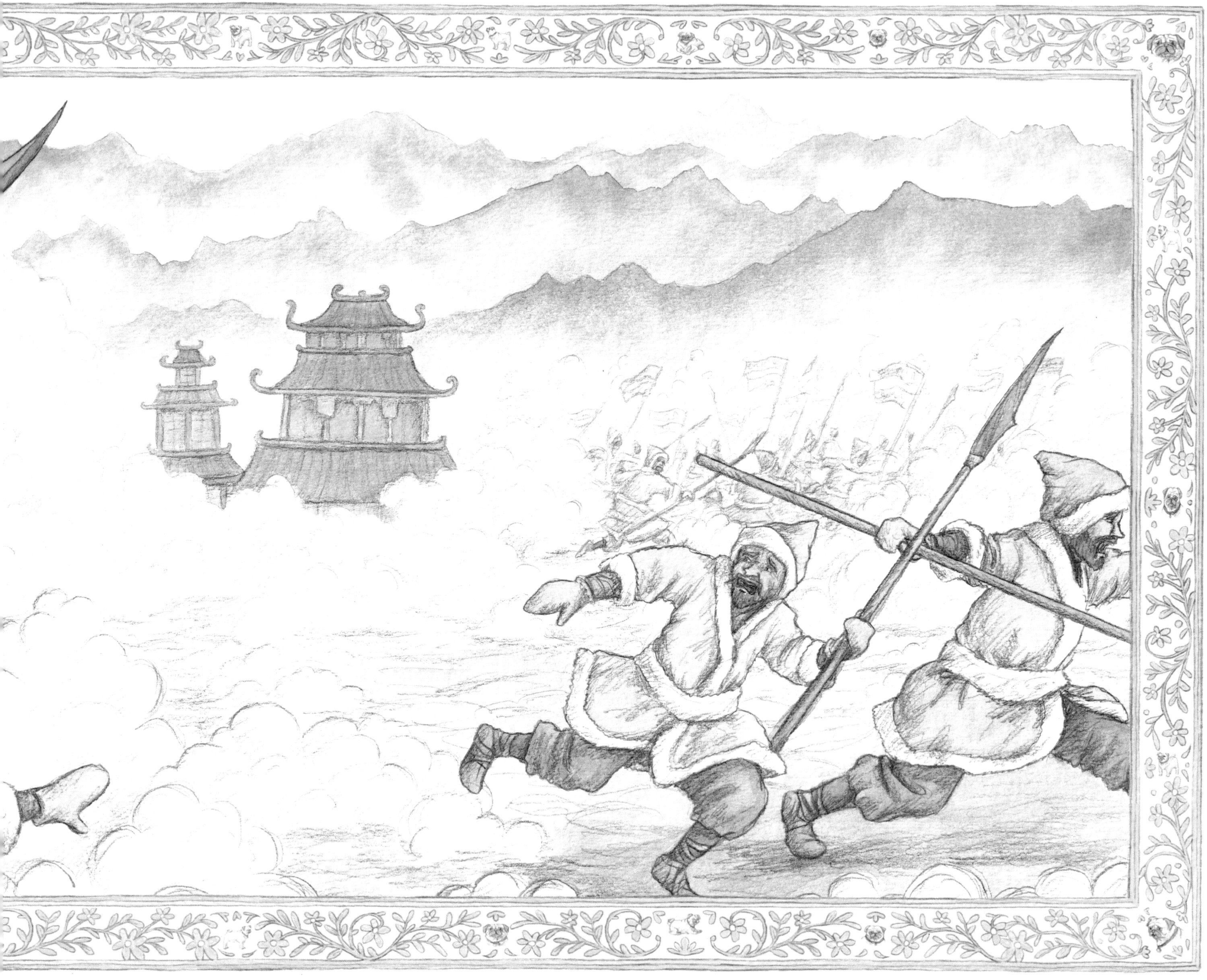

Ferocious. Too bad, because it would have been a good fight to see Genghis go against my ancestor.

The Shang emperor was impressed by my ancestor Ferocious' bravery. More importantly, he was awed by his wisdom. He issued the following decree in the empire: "Henceforth, my servant Ferocious will be known as General Celestial Wisdom, first advisor to the Emperors of China." As was the custom at the time, the emperor's advisors had to be eunuchs so that they would have no worldly concerns other than the emperor. But before General Celestial Wisdom became a eunuch, he was allowed to sire children so that his descendants could advise future generations of emperors. And thus it has been for 3,620 years. Three-hundred generations, the male descendants of General Celestial Wisdom, have sired children before they became eunuchs. General Celestial Wisdom was a scholar/warrior/philosopher, and he advised the Shang emperor for years on how to run the empire of China, the greatest civilization in the world, favored by the gods.

When General Celestial Wisdom died, the Shang emperor suffered great grief. He decreed that forever after the sons of General Celestial, we pugs would be bred to be gentle, small philosophers. For if we were not small, we would end up running the show. We would advise—not rule. Our diminutive size would force us to be most persuasive.

Pugs created the great science of genetics, which persists to this day. We manipulated our genetic code to produce the best breed of dogs in the universe. Unfortunately, the Shang emperor also decreed that the ancestors of General Celestial must be tested by life's adversities like their ancestor, the General. Any pug that was not smaller and more philosophical joined our cousin, the Chinese chow dog, on the way to the dinner table. That motivated us to protect the science of genetics.

We thus learned from 3,620 years of experience that you must be tough and philosophical to triumph over life's adversities. I hope to help my humans, who are my responsibility, to overcome their own adversities.

Our numbers are not great. There are only twenty thousand pugs in the United States today. But what we lack in numbers, we make up for in determination. We pugs are the royalty of the canine world; we are humbled that we have been able to serve mankind for centuries by advising emperors and saving civilizations.

The great Shang Emperor Lung-To awarded his poet pug, my ancestor, Yu Lo, the empire's highest award for achievement, the *Hosiengate*, complete with the belt and the signs of office in 1300 BC. Yu Lo was the Chinese Shakespeare whose poems are still read in today's classrooms. As a young man, Yu Lo would sit on top of a hill and write his poems on rice paper, fold them like little boats, and send them floating down a mountain stream. Fortunately, there was a monastery at the bottom of the hill. A scholar monk found the poems, recognized their worth, and notified the emperor. That is how Yu Lo became poet laureate of China and how his legacy was saved for all mankind. He had a troop of servants to cater to his every need. He rode to the royal hunt in a custom-built red lacquer carriage, encrusted with jade and gilt ornaments. Yu Lo would be carried out to the field to stalk his quarry (mice), for he was a ferocious hunter. After the hunt, he was carried back to the silken cushions of the imperial court where he would compose poems that celebrated love, war, and the wisdom of his Emperor. Not all pugs of the General's line are warriors.

Pompey, another member of my family, was the advisor to William the Silent, the Duke of Orange (1560 AD). The Duke was driving in his carriage to reach his army. He was attacked by Spanish troops who had invaded Holland. Pompey leapt to defend his master's face from a sword blow, shielding him with his own body (don't worry, he had armor), and giving him early warning of the attack. The emperor awarded Pompey his nation's highest award for gallantry in action and had his army march before Pompey and present arms. Pompey continued the pug's martial traditions, winning many awards for valor while writing the greatest histories of Holland's Golden Age. You see, he was named after the great Roman General Pompeius Magnus, conqueror of the Middle Sea, Mithridates, and

9

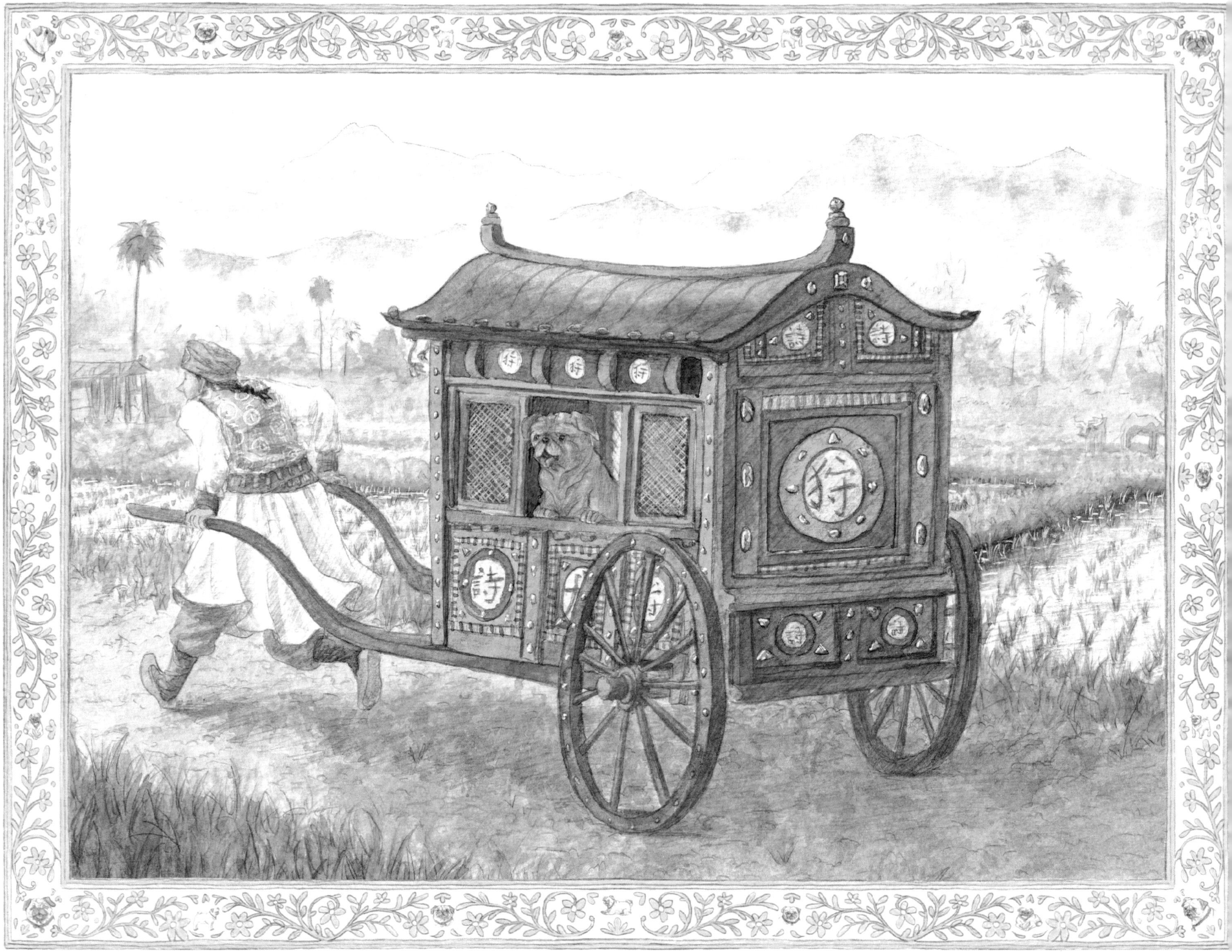

the Land of the Parthians. From that day on, pugs were the official dogs of the House of Orange. When William and Mary ascended the English throne (1700 AD), their pugs' collars were threaded with orange ribbons.

The Spanish line of my family was led by Luicentes de Goya, the pug of Spanish court painter Francisco Goya (1780 AD). Early in the career of the great painter, before Napoleon's invasion and the disasters of war, he painted Luicentes in scenes of light and happiness. I believe it was Luicentes' death, and the bestial tragedy of the war with the French, that drove Goya to his dark paintings. It is the unfortunate tendency of our human masters to become too attached to their pugs, for when we die, as we must, they feel that the warmth of the sun has left their lives.

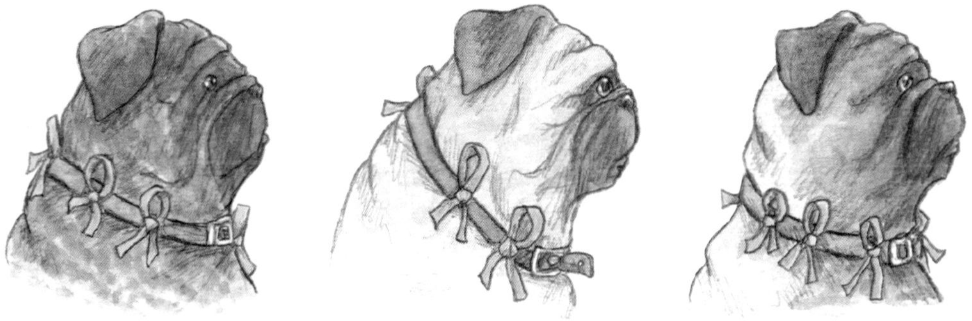

In Saxony, the Freemasons espoused democracy (ca.1820 AD), and the rights of Freeman to govern their own destiny. My ancestor Gerhard Mopes created the Society of Mopeshounds, and the pug was the symbol of the Freemasons. The great craftsman Knadler (ca. 1730 AD), an artist in Augustus the Strong's court, created the Meissen porcelain factory and immortalized my ancestor Gerhard in hard-paste porcelain. When the evil pope excommunicated all Freemasons from the Catholic Church, they declared themselves the Mopesorder of The Order of the Pug. I am convinced that Gerhard's ancestor,

Luthorius, gave his master, Martin Luther, advice when he nailed the ninety-five Theses that became the Protestant Church to a cathedral door (ca. 1517).

Marie Antoinette brought a pug to France in May of 1770. Her name was Ma Cher, my long-dead distant cousin. When she was a young, frivolous pug, she liked to pretend she was a shepherdess. She did not have a mean bone in her little body, yet she was guillotined. When the rebels led the revolt against Marie's husband, Louis XVI, they demanded brown bread. Ma Cher, with her mistress, Marie, led a procession of carts filled with the white bread, the best bread in the world that was served at Versailles to feed the rebels. Ma Cher said, "Let them eat cake," for that was what white bread was called in France. Your best intentions can be turned by evil people, like TV news writers and hosts, into propaganda that can be used against you. At the end of her life, Ma Cher changed and became a very serious pug and worked with a serious Marie to establish democracy in France. For this crime, she was led alone to the guillotine, separated from her beloved Marie.

But, Ma Cher's daughter was Fortune, the pug of the divine Empress Josephine, married to Napoleon (March 1796). I am convinced Napoleon was the reincarnation of our ancestor, General Celestial Wisdom, a pug reborn as a human. To establish the pecking order of life, Fortune bit Napoleon when he tried to climb into Josephine's bed on their wedding night. This did not deter Napoleon, yet he greatly valued Fortune's advice. In fact, Code Napoleon should be called Code Fortune. Napoleon and Fortune became co-conspirators since Napoleon hid his love letters to Josephine under Fortune's collar, and he delivered them when she was imprisoned in the prison Les Carmes in 1794 during the madness of the French Revolution.

Of course, when the Iron Duke Wellington captured many of Napoleon's favorite possessions in June 1816, he also seized La Fortuna, Fortune's daughter. He gave her to Queen Victoria, and she gave birth to many pugs:

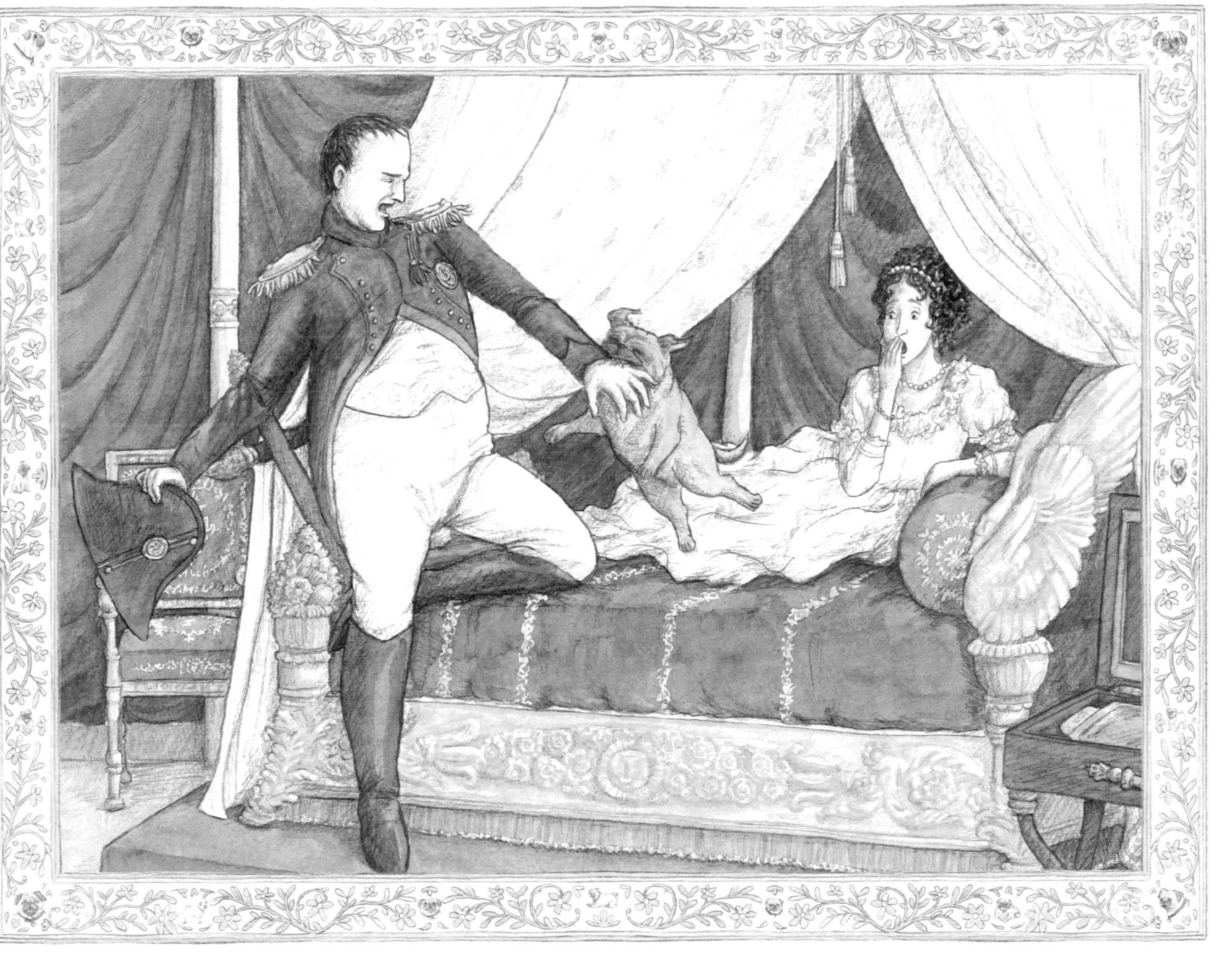

Olga, Pedro, Nicola, Fatima, Venus, and, of course, the great Bosco. It was Bosco who spent most of his life in the Highlands and considered himself the Rob Roy of pugs that helped Victoria create Pax Britannia, a period of peace and creativity, which rivaled that of Pax Romana. My human masters have bought me Queen Victoria's bronze pug sculpture of Bosco, and it is among my most prized possessions.

Oh, yes, we pugs have a history, but it is a history of gravitas and duty to mankind. Pugs in China were known as Lo Chiang—Sze or Foo. Foo dogs were the mythical dragons that guarded the Celestial Empire. The Roman motto *Mutteum in Paro* refers to the breed of pug *a lot in a little.* The wrinkles on a pug's forehead spell out the Chinese character for *prince*.

My personal favorite among all my ancestors is Trump (ca. 1745 AD). Trump came to England before his French niece, La Fortuna. Trump was the special person in the life of the great painter William Hogarth. It is Trump who sits in the lap of Hogarth for his self-portrait. It was Trump who taught Hogarth to laugh at mankind's weaknesses, and weep as well. For the legacy of pugs is to laugh and to weep.

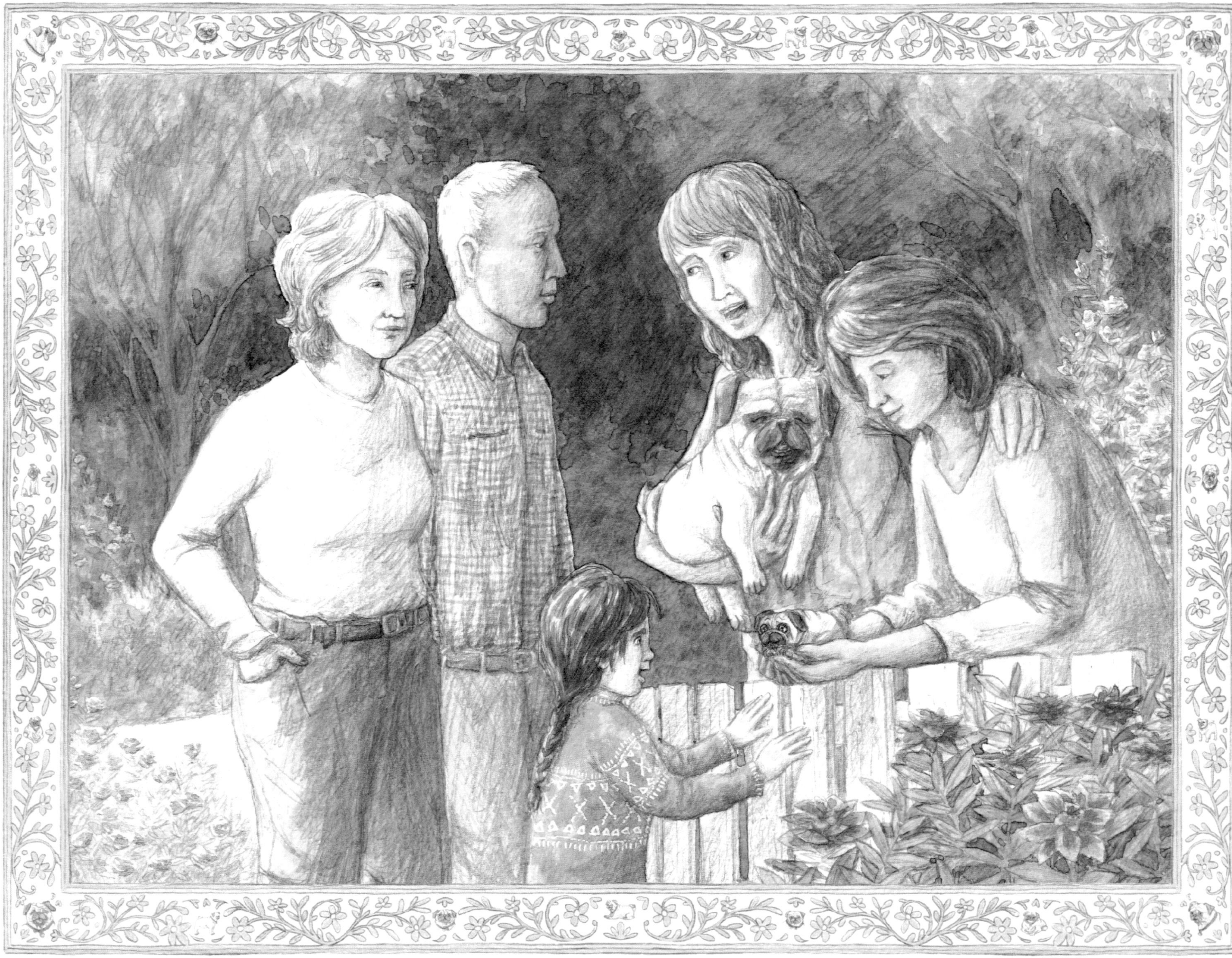

CHAPTER III
MY FIRST FAMILY

My mother's family consisted of two famous female pug breeders who bred pugs of the Sterling line, those related to General Celestial Wisdom. These women loved each other very much, but this upset many of their neighbors who felt that women should not love other women.

Pugs know better than this. Pugs love everyone. If pugs ruled the world, there would never be wars. All pugs know that any disagreement can be resolved by polite conversation over a very good dinner.

My mother was so lovable that she taught the neighbors that they should not judge others just because they were different. In time, the neighbors came to love the two women and their families of pugs.

My mother set a good example for me, Stanley the Pug. She taught me always to respect differences. The more different people are, the more you can learn, if you ignore your prejudices.

CHAPTER IV

WALKING TALL–A PERSON'S A PERSON NO MATTER HOW SMALL

I left my mother's family and adopted my own human family, the Newhalls. Humans need a pug to look after them.

My family has a mommy and a daddy, and two giant boys, my brothers, Ashton and Adair. Each brother is six-feet, four-inches tall. I have told those big boys that they should become more philosophical, or some emperor may choose to shrink them. But they do not listen to me.

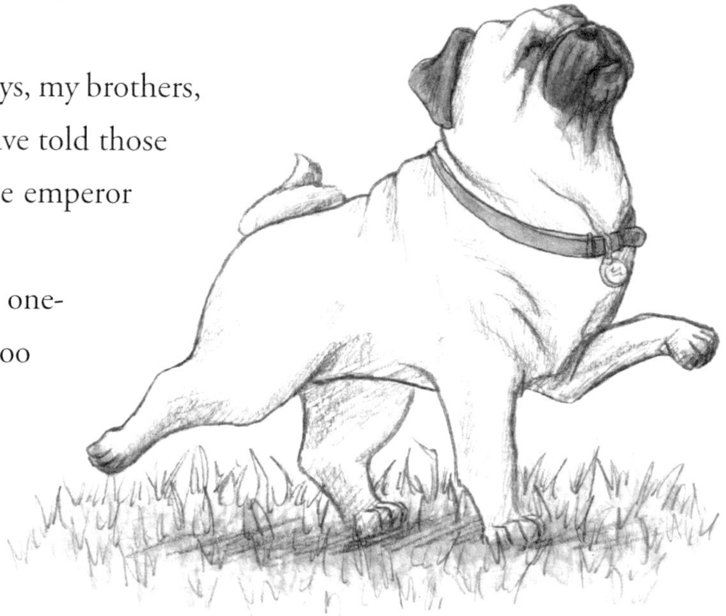

My family also includes Ramses, a Siamese cat, Morgan, a one-hundred-and-twenty-pound male German shepherd who has too much testosterone, and Edwina, an eighty-pound female shepherd who is very gentle. I, Stanley the Pug, am only fourteen pounds and hardly stand above Morgan's paws. We animals held an election to see who would be top dog (or cat). It was my fortune to win.

But Morgan the shepherd, like many small-minded humans, called for a recount. I won again. This upset Morgan, and he decided to protest. If I had been president of the United States, he would have tried to impeach me. Poor Morgan did not know that my ancestor was General Celestial Wisdom, the great Chinese warrior.

Mommy and Daddy took me out to the lawn. I was only one year old, and Morgan was three. I was tiny. Morgan was very big. All bullies that you meet in life are very big. But if you have the courage to confront them like General Celestial Wisdom did when he defeated the eighteen-foot Northern Barbarian bear in mortal combat, you realize that the bigger they are, the harder they fall. Bad Morgan chased me around the lawn three times until I feigned exhaustion and lay on my back.

19

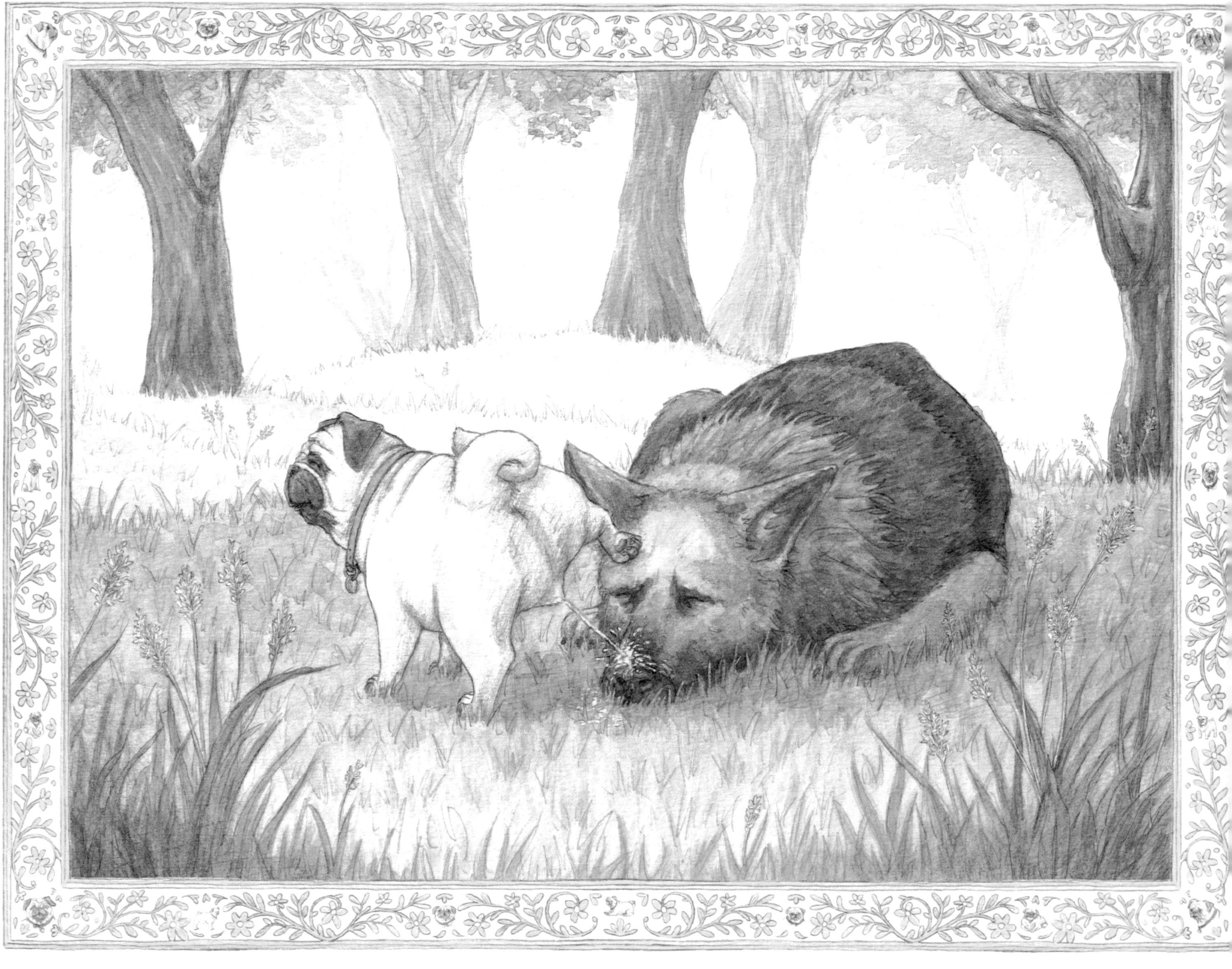

Morgan thought he had won and was about to mark me as his territory. I bit down upon the lower part of Morgan's anatomy, which he intended to use to mark me. Morgan howled and dragged me around the lawn. But I held on until Morgan collapsed on the lawn. I then marked my territory on his face and strutted away.

Now you may think it's not correct for one pug or person to pee on another. But pugs just call things as they are. We pugs are modest, courteous, smart, and brave. We don't need others telling us what to do, and we never tell other breeds or people what they must do. I leave that to toy poodles who prance around with pom poms on their feet and head.

Morgan and I are now good friends. Pugs never hold a grudge, and now I help old Morgan around the house. I am his doctor and his nurse. We have learned to respect each other's virtues despite Morgan's testosterone.

It was important for Morgan, and humans, to learn that a person's a person no matter how small. My human brothers learned that when you are being bullied, you must walk tall and carry a big stick—a good lesson for human children.

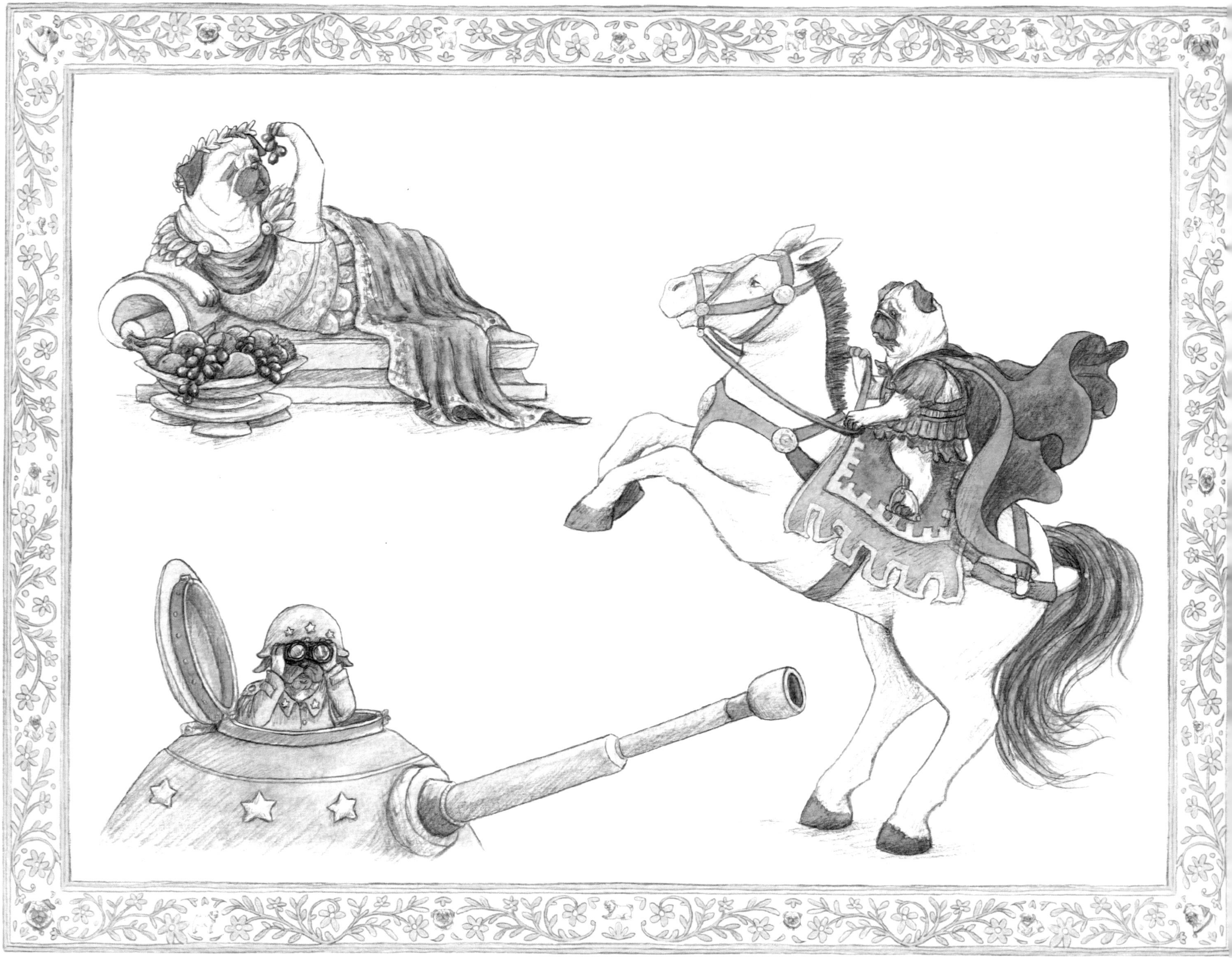

CHAPTER V
DREAM THE IMPOSSIBLE DREAM

Pugs sleep most of the day and night. During sleep, I have many dreams, which for me are healthy fantasies that help me combat life's trials.

I dreamt that I was Pug the Great, one of Alexander the Great's companions who conquered the world and made one society from different races and enacted laws that we still use.

I dreamt that I was Pug Caesar who helped my human, Julius, conquer the Gauls. I fought with him in the Battle of Alicia, where we defeated Vercingetorex and the Gauls. While Caesar stormed Vercingetorex's fort, I infiltrated it and set up a bar that offered free wine, caviar, and foie gras to all Vercingetorex's bare-chested barbarian warriors with skin that was painted blue. They were served by beautiful bare-chested barbarian women. By the time Caesar's legionnaires entered the fort, all Vercingetorex's warriors were either drunk or off chasing women. After all, they were French men under their blue skins. I came, I saw, I conquered, and after we defeated the Gauls, the Divine Julius and I created Rome, which is the greatest of all civilizations.

I dreamt that I was Patton Pug who defeated the Nazi Germans in the deserts of North Africa.

Dreams are not reality, but they do teach us to have high aspirations. Dream well. Do great things.

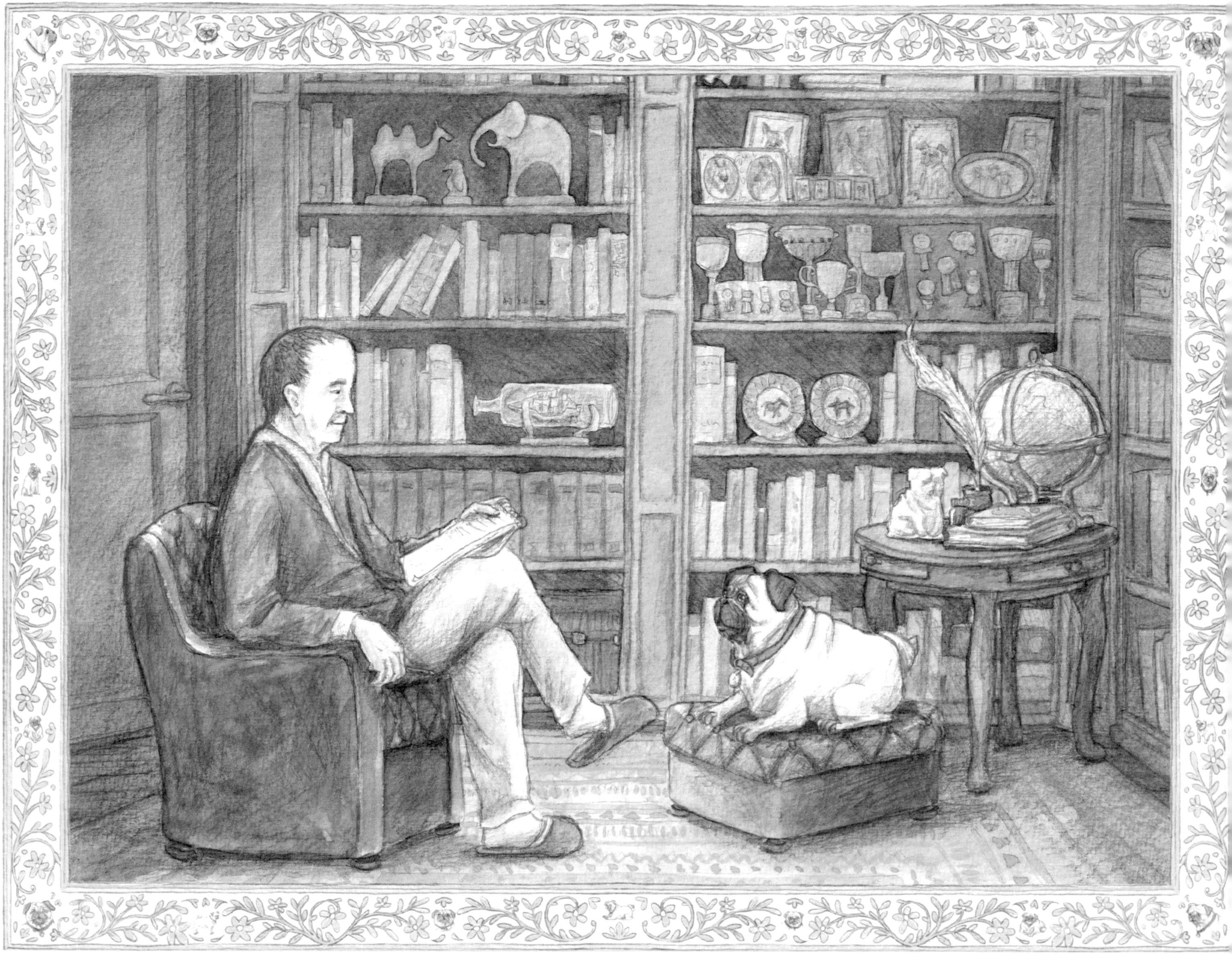

CHAPTER VI
STAND BY YOUR MAN

My daddy is an old venture capitalist. He is more than sixty years old. Over his career, he has been part of a partnership that has started over twelve hundred companies, some of which have changed the world. But in his old age, Daddy had the wind knocked out of his sails just when he thought he should be sailing off into the sunset of life. There was a great craziness in the world, the Bubble, which claimed we were in a new economy (a new world order) where the rules that my dad learned over the past sixty years had no meaning. That was the first setback. Then, he found out that two of the companies he had helped start were run by very evil men who took advantage of their investors and the people who had helped build their companies. That was the second setback. The third that went wrong was when he was asked to retire from the venture capital he founded. It was, as they say, the perfect storm. Dad became very disillusioned and sad.

I would sit every night and remind him that the pugs overcame adversity to become great philosophers. How you recover from defeats is more important than all your triumphs. The warmth of a pug's love restored his soul, and Dad discovered that he was never too old to learn and try new things. I am happy to have played a small part in teaching him this lesson. He is now happy and has had three careers. He was a warrior. Then he was a venture capitalist. Now he is an author. That is not bad for an old human who was encouraged and aided by his pug.

CHAPTER VII
CONVERSATION

One thing that my mother taught me is that no matter how shy you are, it is important to look whomever you are speaking to in the eye; speak up and express your opinions with grace and modesty. After all, it was pugs who taught humans how to be polite people.

Every Thanksgiving and Christmas holiday my parents place me on a chair at the dining room table and tie a napkin around my neck. Since it is a special holiday, I must hold up my end of the family. I nod when spoken to. I bark softly to the person on my left and my right, and try to be amusing and charming. They always seem to understand me.

The funny thing is that you do not need to speak to have a conversation. Doctors say that 95 percent of communication is not verbal. It is what a person's eyes tell you about them and what they are thinking—body language. But whatever the truth, when a little person is around a big person, by all means, communicate. Don't be shy. Observe those around you and learn. To learn every day is the way to knowledge, according to the great book, *The Way of Pug*.

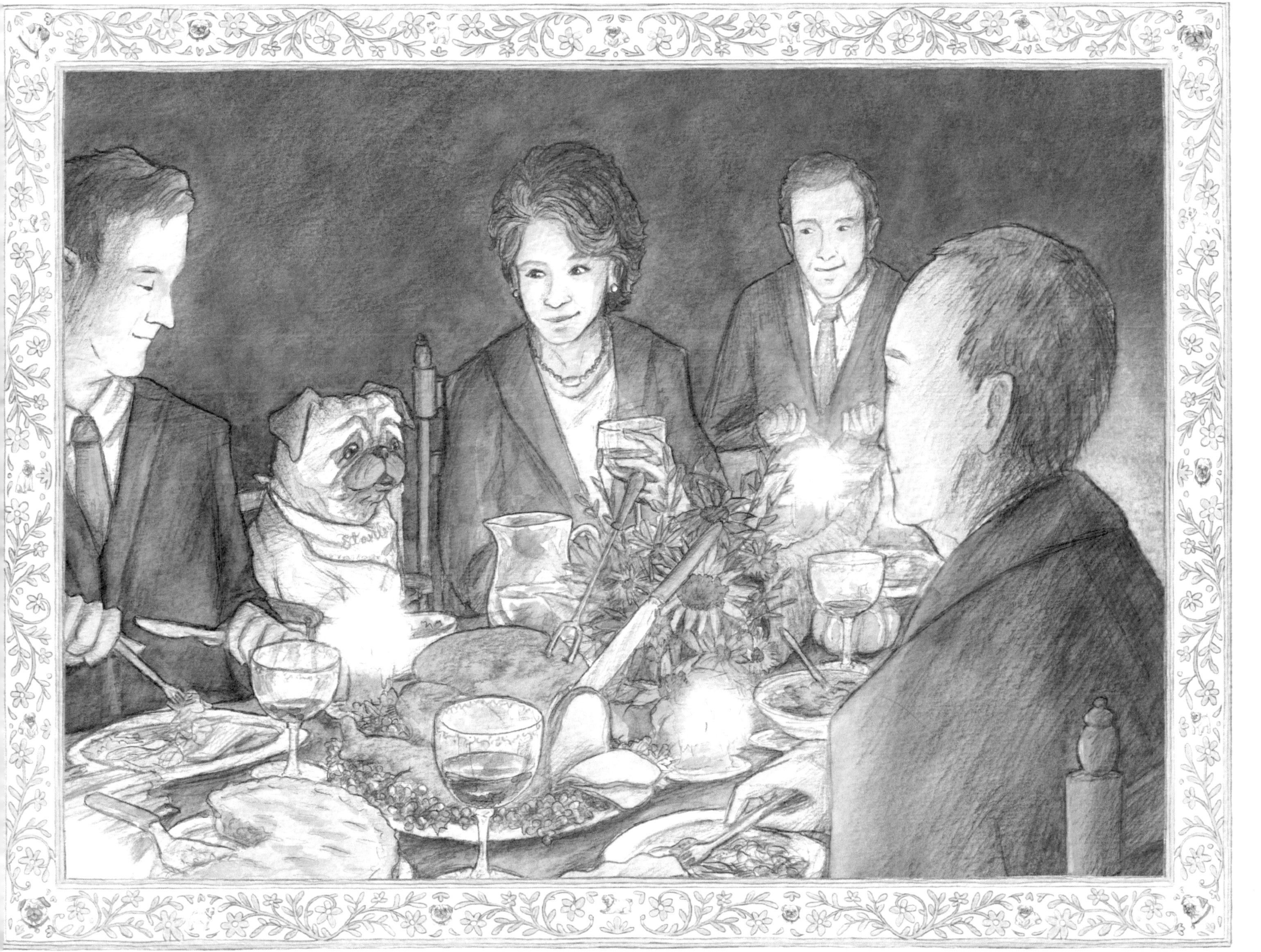

CHAPTER VIII
MOMMY'S BOY (SHARING A LIFE)

Like most pugs, I am a mommy's boy. I love my human mommy the most because she loves me the most. But moms, like all humans, have problems no matter how smart they are. My mommy spent the past twenty years of her life raising boys, my human brothers. She watched all their games and school plays, took them to the doctor, and stayed up all night with them when they were sick.

When her boys left her nest, she thought she lost her purpose. She needed a serious amount of pug-hugging. I told her that she would never stop being a mother. The boys would need her advice forever, but now was her time to help other children. So, she became a trustee of a school for the learning disabled, an organization that helped women who suffered from domestic violence, and a school that helped children with Down syndrome, the sweetest and most innocent children on earth. Now she is teaching her grandchildren how to be good humans.

She was living the advice that my mother pug gave me growing up; you are always happiest when you are helping others.

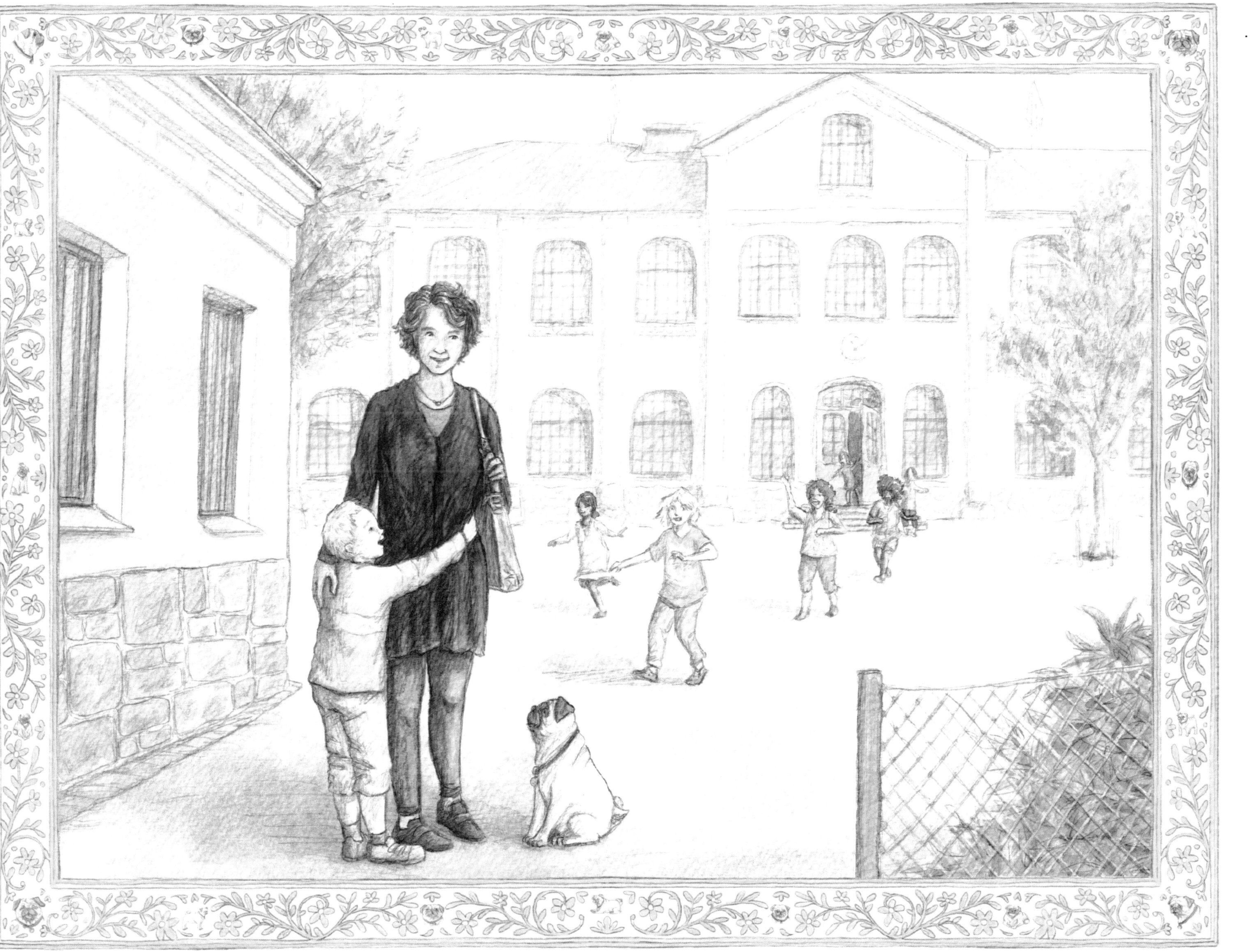

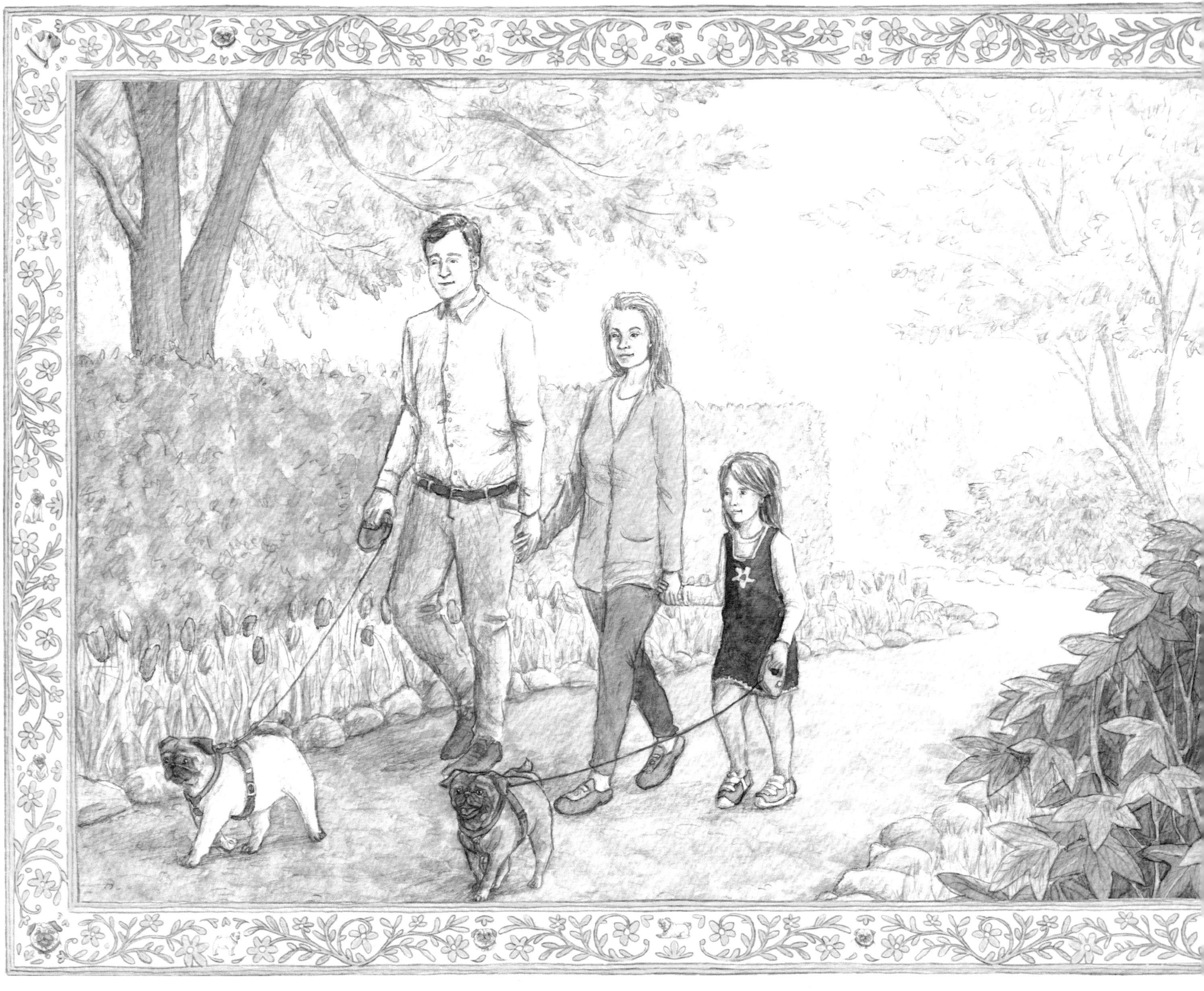

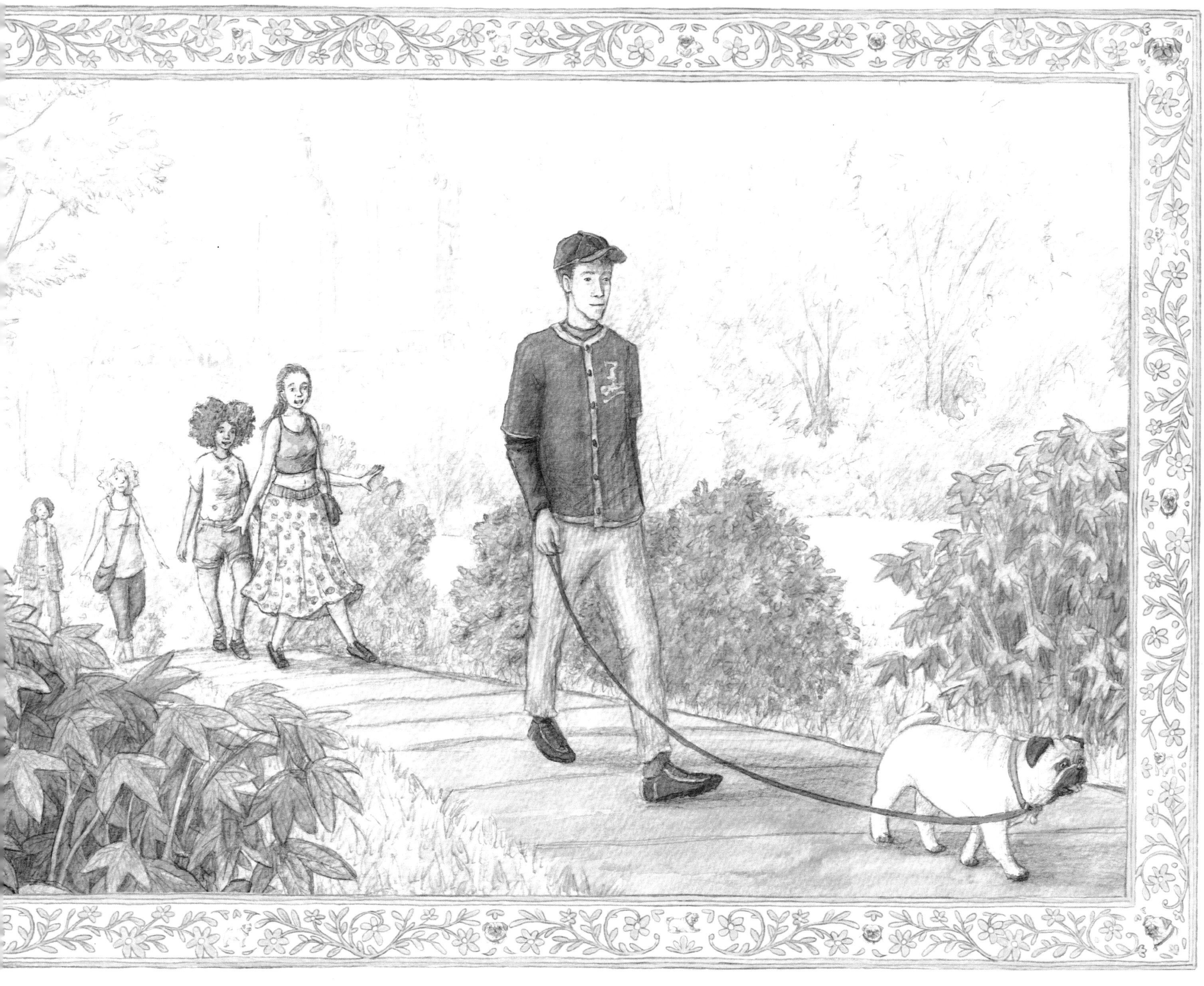

CHAPTER IX
MY BROTHERS

My brothers are Ashton and Adair. Like all young male humans and German shepherd dogs, they possess too much testosterone to think like the great philosophers. Thank the Shang emperor for making us eunuchs, ensuring that pugs would not be bothered by the trivial pursuits of too much testosterone. But my mom would be mad at me if I neutered her sons.

My oldest brother, Ashton, is a wonderful young human, but like many of his kind, he is too focused on himself. This is where I come in. I had to teach him that more joy comes from being focused on others than oneself. Several years ago, Ashton brought a beautiful and intelligent young woman (Becky) to our house. This was the first step toward civilization. I sat beside Becky and extolled Ashton's virtues, except for his failure to brush his teeth and shave his ugly beard. The next thing I know, they are married.

Beautiful Becky had a beautiful daughter from a prior marriage named Aley. I taught Ashton how to play with this young girl by taking daddy-daughter getaways and focusing only on her. I taught him to see the joy of her smile. Aley loves me, and I love Aley. She hugs me every time she sees me. Ashton and Becky had two more children, the beautiful Sydney and Brantley. I teach all three girls at the same time. It does not worry me since girls are easier to teach than boys.

The final lesson I taught Ashton was most difficult. I had to get Ashton to obtain a pet of his own. You see, when Ashton was young, he never fed his pets because he was too busy having fun. However, a married man's fun should come from his family—and pugs. After many discussions, Ashton agreed to invite the pugs, Bennett and A.J., to join his family. The civilization of young Ashton is now complete. He has his family, and he is much happier taking care of them than playing baseball or computer games. But, then again, Ashton was never good at baseball.

My younger brother, Adair, was another story. He was very good at baseball. He played varsity for the University of Pennsylvania, and they defeated a school in New Jersey called Princeton Juvenile Detention Center. Adair is handsome, six-foot-four-inches, athletic, brilliant, and hard working. He has already been part of starting two new companies in the pharmaceutical industry. Someday, he will be wealthy. He is so kind. He always fed dogs and cats.

His problem is that he wants so much to be in love that most young women do not seem to like him. That is the way young human females are. Before the age of thirty, they like men who treat them poorly. After thirty, they like men who treat them well.

I have called some mature and very wise women I respect for advice, to see if they know any young women of merit. They told me to find an intelligent woman who will appreciate Adair.

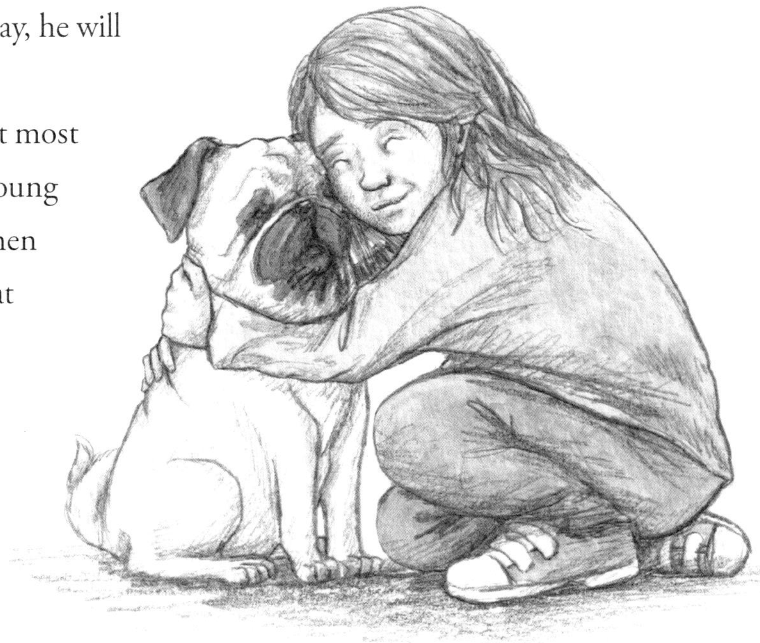

I went to visit Adair at the University of Virginia where he was studying at Darden to get his MBA. I took him for walks on the famous lawn, which was designed by Thomas Jefferson. You see, pugs are serious chick magnets. On one of our walks, he met the beautiful Kathryn, the blonde, super smart lawyer. Now they are married, and a baby is on the way. I am sure he brings her breakfast in bed every morning.

The only problem is that they invited Oliver, a Cavalier King Charles spaniel, to join their family. Oliver is okay, but like all fluffy things whose primary job is only to look beautiful, he cannot control his bodily functions. Ugh! But Oliver is a happy soul that brings delight to Adair and his family. We pugs will miss him when he is gone. I have granted Oliver the title *Honorary Pug*.

CHAPTER X
THE PATH TO GOD

Lorna is my Jamaican mother. She loves me. She is also a very good person, a member of our family who has taken care of us for forty years, making sure our house is clean, we have food, and our home is a happy place. But even pugs can be messy and spill their food, spill their water, and occasionally mess in the house when people forget to take them outside. Lorna sometimes becomes angry and then worries that she will not go to heaven. But, of all the humans I have met on Earth, Lorna is most like a pug. Her life is spent helping others and knowing that helping others is fun and is the road to heaven.

So I have to tell Lorna a big secret—pugs are angels without wings. We get wings when we go to heaven. This angel to be has already told God about Lorna's goodness, and it will be my job to personally escort her to heaven when the time comes. I once heard a story. God was standing on the Earth amid all his glory, having just created the universe, the world, and Adam and Eve. Lightening flashed, thunder rolled, the ocean crashed, and God beheld his handiwork. He had given a name to everything in his creation.

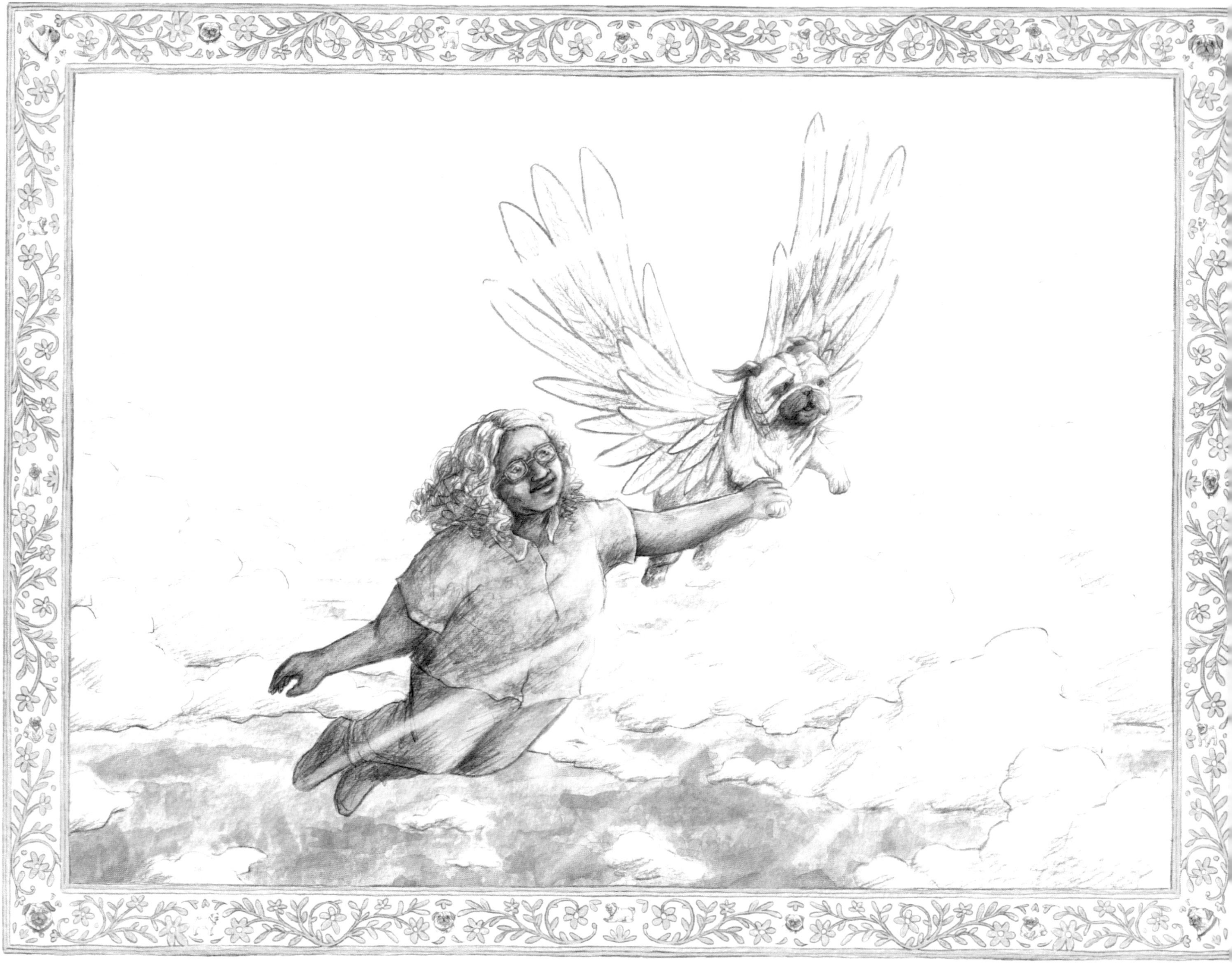

Suddenly, out of the underbrush, bedraggled by rain, lost and lonely, comes a little pug. In a small voice, the pug asks God, "Lord of all creatures on Earth, you have named them all but me. Lord, what am I to be called?" The Lord God looked down and his eyes filled with compassion. He said, "You are last but not least. Do not worry little one, for you are meek, gentle, and very good. You shall have my name spelled backward—D O G."

So don't worry, Lorn, I have connections with the Big Guy.

CHAPTER XI
MY GIRLFRIEND

Hanna, a young woman from the Ukraine, is also part of our family. She has taken care of us for seven years. She is driven to work very hard. She works all day and then goes to school at night. She was a registered nurse in the Ukraine, but her degree is not recognized in the United States. She is now retraining herself to be an accountant. She, too, is a very good person. She sends all her money to help her family in the Ukraine. Perhaps we could all learn a lesson from this. We all should help others who are less fortunate than ourselves.

I am trying hard to convince Hannah to have more fun. Pugs and humans must work hard but have fun. All work and no play makes boys and girls and pugs dull.

I introduced her to her husband, and now she has children and has lots of fun with her family. But she works even harder now, as we all must.

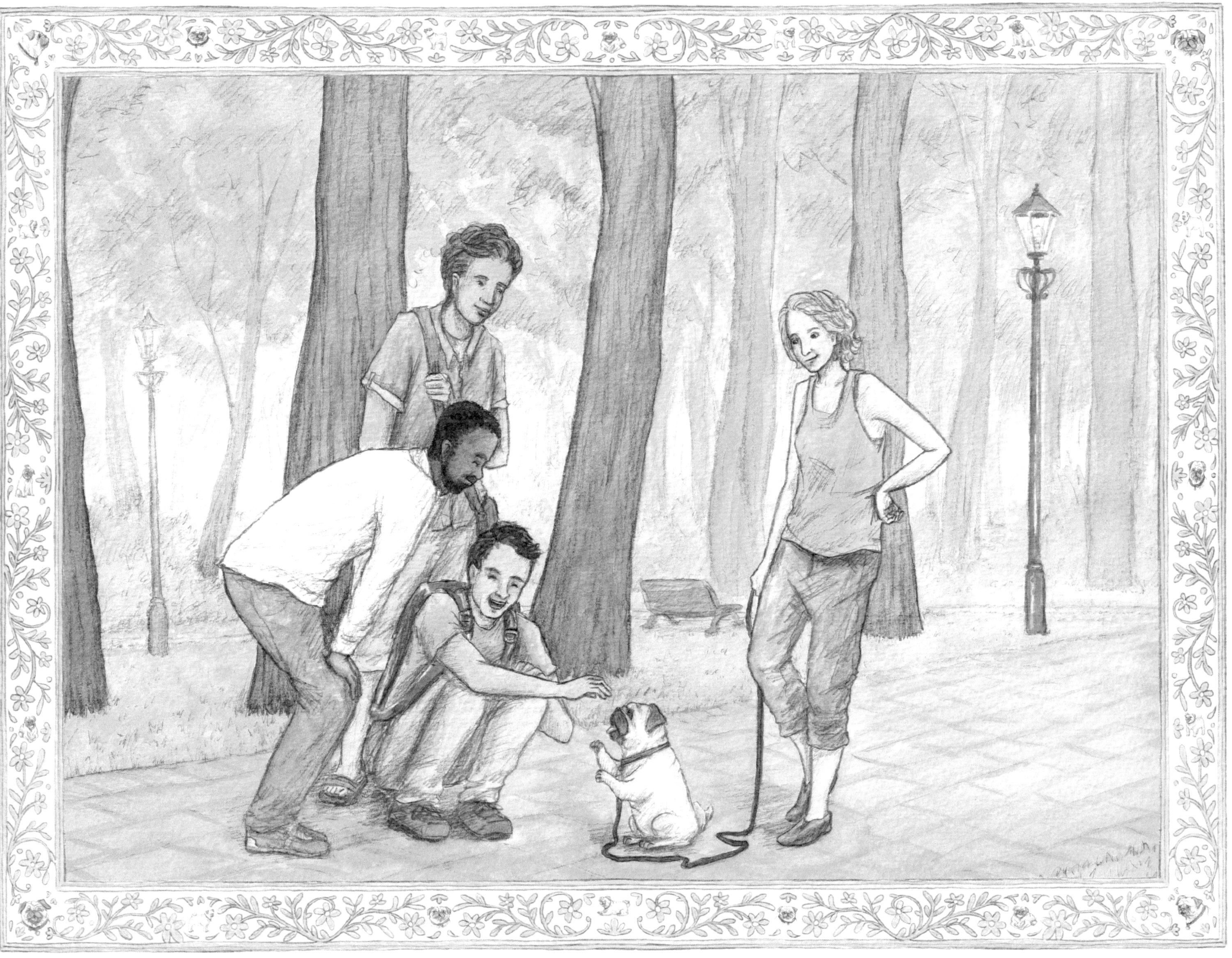

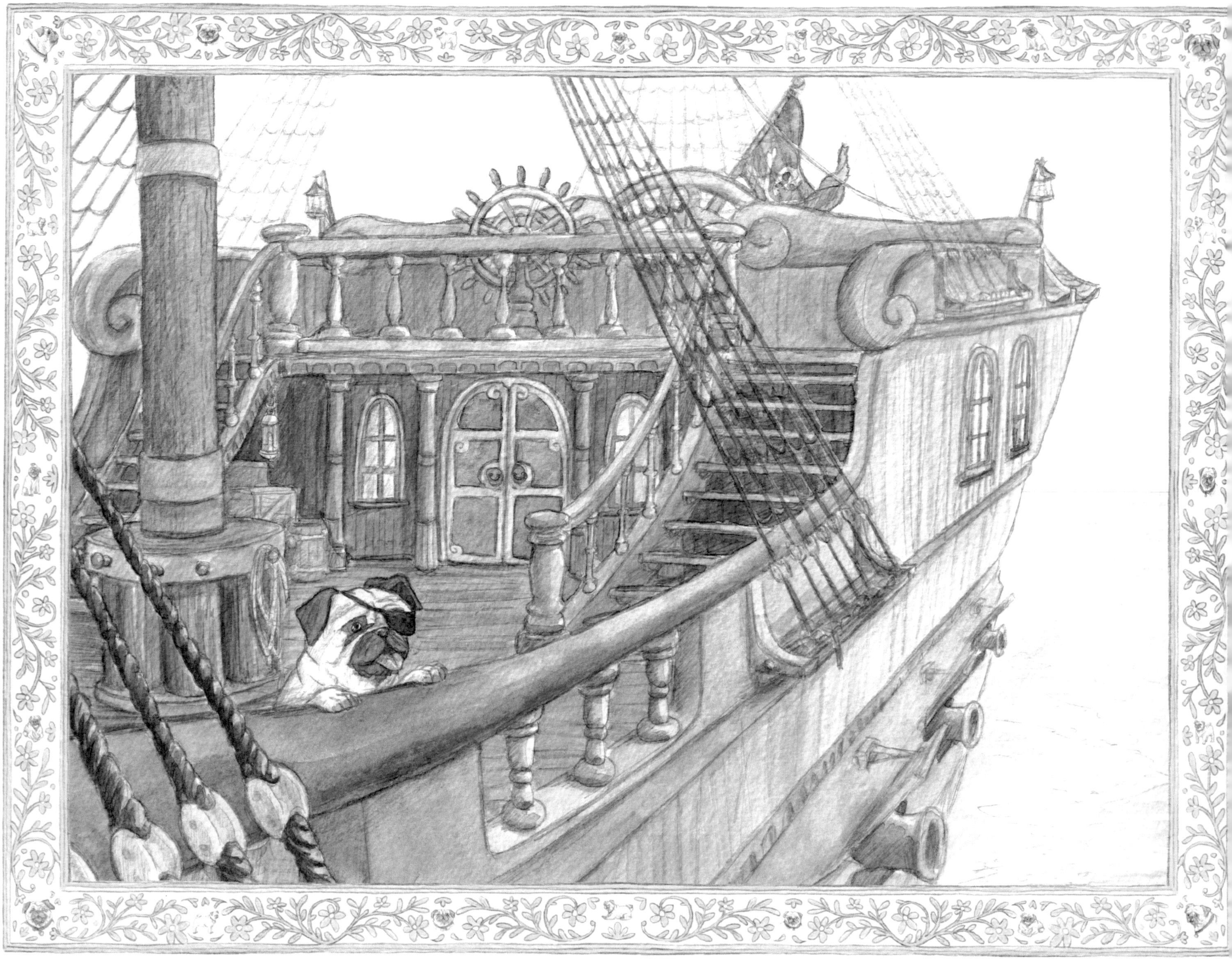

CHAPTER XII
NEVER TOO OLD

As I approached my final years, I faced an end-of-life crisis. Pugs have disadvantages. Our eyes protrude in front of our faces. While Mommy and Daddy were on vacation, I got an ear infection. It itched terribly, and, stupidly, I scratched my eye while I was trying to reach my ear. By the time Mom and Dad returned home, my eye was badly infected and had to be removed. You see, in life, we often do the most damage to ourselves.

So now, I am a one-eyed pug. General Celestial always said that a good pug can always find a way to turn bad news into good news. I have bought an eye patch and have been offered a major part in the sequel to *Pirates of the Caribbean* called *Pugs Pirates of the Caribbean.* I may even become a movie star, although I doubt it, since it's a bit too much attention focused on someone who acts rather than does. Too many movie stars are just poorly educated actors who like to tell everyone else what to do. I guess I will not take that part after all. I am much too smart.

I want to set an example for my brothers. The measure of a man is how he recovers from defeats, not how he behaves in his triumphs. A measure of a man—or a pug—is what he does for the world. It's never about acting a part.

CHAPTER XIII
RAMSES THE CAT

Ramses was a Siamese cat. Some people found him exotic because he is from another country. Siamese cats descended from Bast and Bastet, the cat gods of the Egyptians and sisters Wajet and Sekhment, the lion goddesses. Ramses was one of my best teachers in life.

Although many breeds look down on dogs that sleep with cats, Ramses and I slept together, morning and night, until my friend Ramses died. Ramses was much older than me. Siamese cats have lived many lives and carry the wisdom of many lives with them. Pugs also carry the wisdom of many lives.

Ramses was a great magician. He could conjure the temples of Egypt before us. He could call the great philosophers of history before us to debate what was necessary to help humans to live today. I called upon Buddha, Lao Tsu, and many other Asian philosophers. I also called upon Aristotle, Sophocles, and a few other Greeks to get different opinions. Different opinions are good. Ramses called the Gods of Egypt Isis, Osiris, Bast, and Bastet. It was a lively debate. So, I would like to ask everyone to remember my friend Ramses the cat for one minute of silence. Teachers must always be honored. The secrets of the past that we discovered will be handed down to future pugs and future Siamese cats. The keys to the future are always in the past.

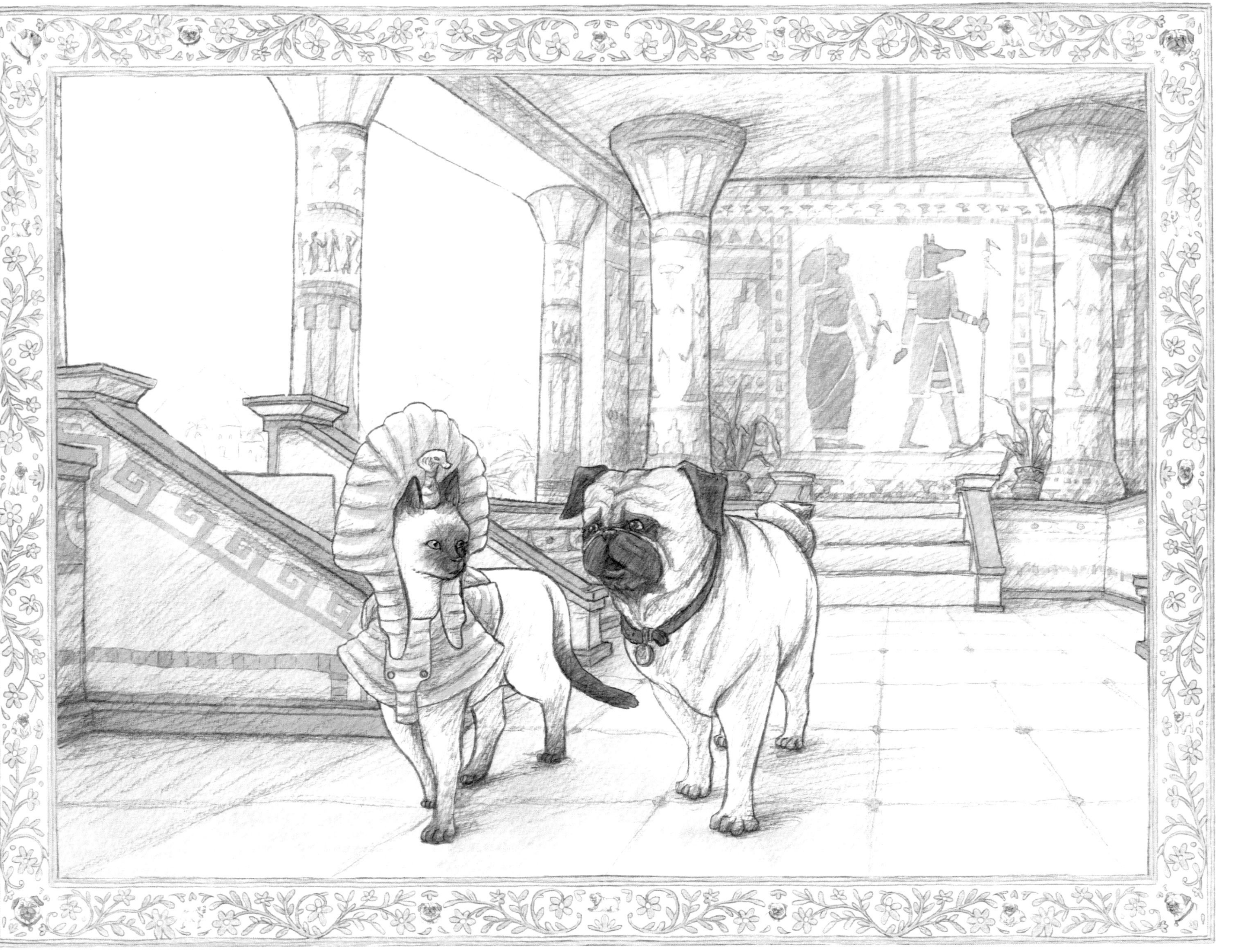

CHAPTER XIV
GRAVE GOODS AND HONORS IN LIFE

I must digress for a moment to talk about grave goods, that which have been collected and given to me to honor my service to my family. They are primarily gifts from my family and friends to me. The grass crown was the highest military award in ancient Rome. It was given to a Roman general whose personal courage and bravery saved the lives of a legion in battle. It could only be awarded by the centurions, the iron professionals of Rome's armies that led cohorts into battle. Centurions, the soldiers who do the real fighting, always know more about courage than the generals. It was made only of grass, not gold. My grave goods are my grass crown, although they are quite beautiful. They are the gifts of my humans to honor the House of Pug. Honors in life are wonderful to receive, but remember when you get them to not let them go to your head. *Sic Gloria transit mundi,* an old Roman saying that means, Glories of the earth are fleeting.

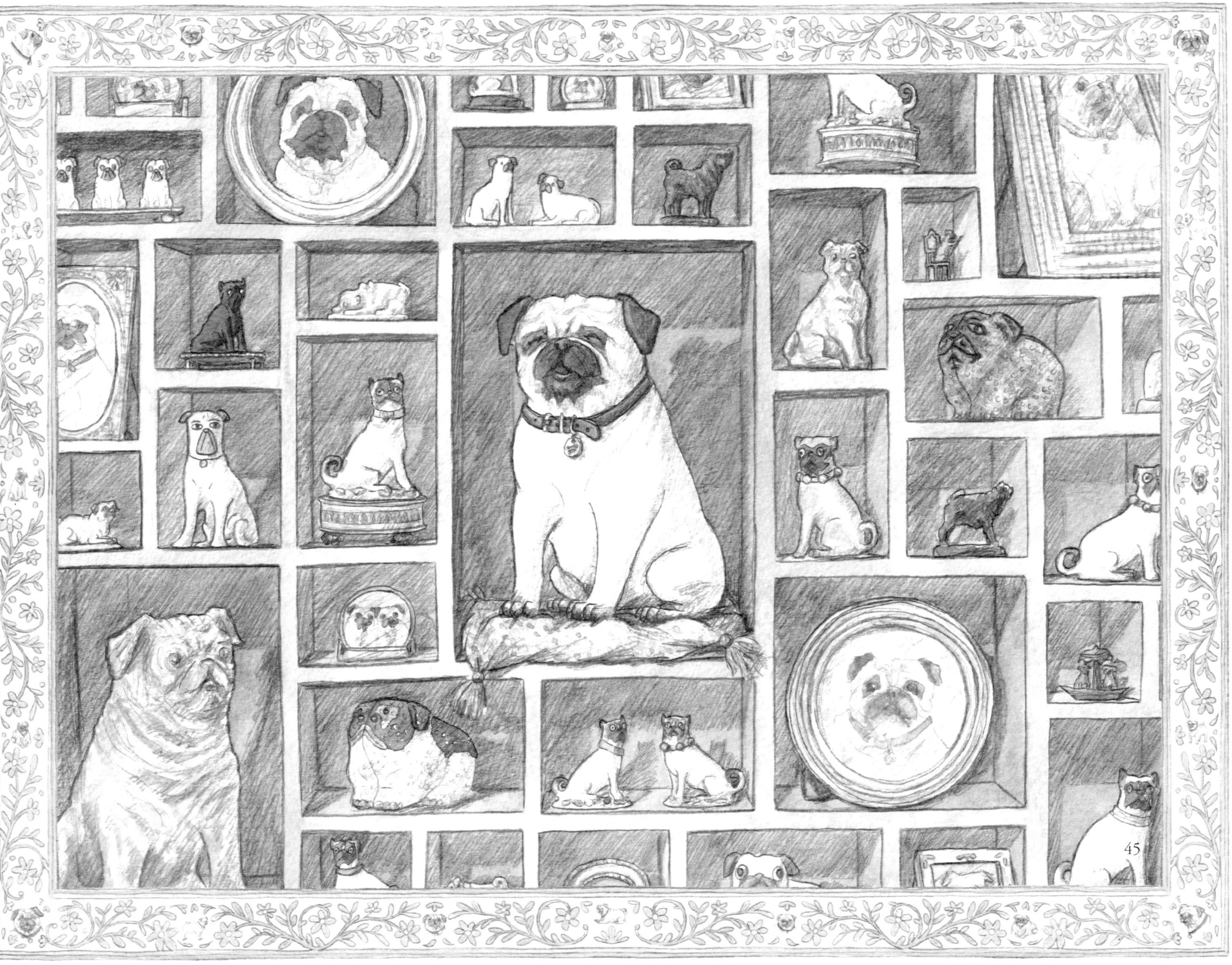

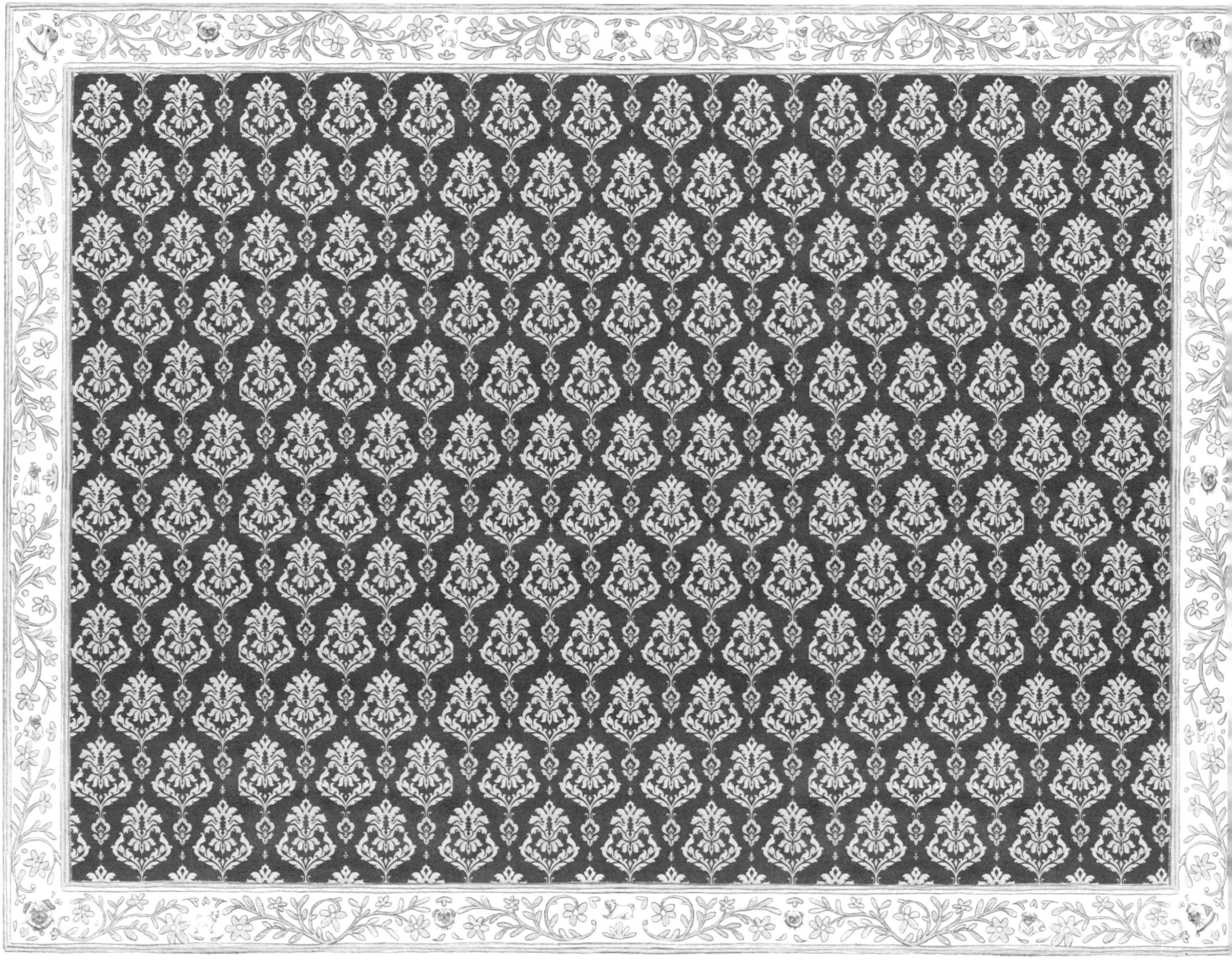

CHAPTER XV
MY FRIEND THE ARTIST

All pugs know that art and beauty are the part of life that restoreth the soul. It is through art that we learn more about ourselves and come to understand our souls. One of the ways we know that God exists is because He has given us art.

Ramses, the Egyptian cat, always told me that it was important to surround yourself with art, so that in the afterlife, we will have companions. King Tut of Egypt had beautiful grave goods made by the greatest artists of his time to go with him for all eternity. Ramses laughed and called me *King Mutt*, and he said I should have grave goods, so art will always surround me, even when I die. Unfortunately, Chinese pugs know that Egyptian cats get too caught up with their own mortality.

In this case, I disagreed with my teacher. But Ramses persuaded my mommy and daddy. For years they have been hiring the best artists to prepare my grave goods. There are two beautiful silver sculptures, each five pounds of sitting Stanleys. There is a life-sized painting of Stanley, Ramses, Morgan, and Winnie. There are five oil paintings of Stanley, numerous watercolors, two life-sized bronze Stanleys, and hundreds of items of pug paraphernalia.

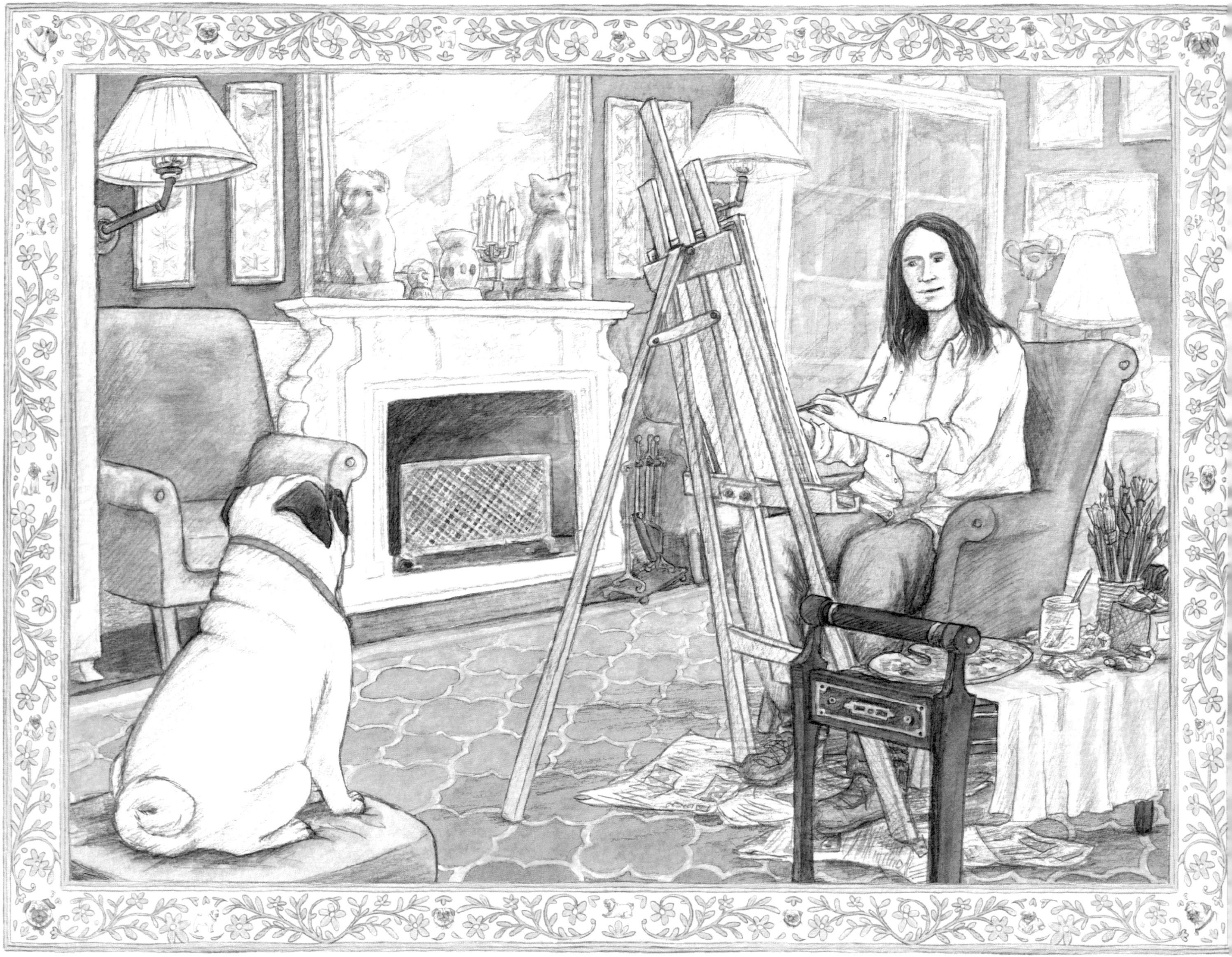

One of the artists, Constance Payne, is my good friend who painted several of my portraits. We have had many conversations about the meaning of art. Constance advised me that grave goods are for ancient Egyptians. The record of Stanley's life belongs to his family and mankind. She said, "Art is for the living, not for the dead." Everyone should be generous in life and death, and I have left my art to my family and the world, not so they will remember me, but rather so they will remember what the ancestors of General Celestial Wisdom stand for. Constance has told me that she will tell my story so that others can benefit from the wisdom that we pugs have garnered throughout the ages. Her paintings of me capture my soul just as the great Leonardo da Vinci captured the soul of Mona Lisa in her smile.

CHAPTER XVI
THE LEGACY OF THE MEEK PUG STANLEY

Remember, your purpose is to help your human family.

Be tough, be philosophical, and triumph over life's adversities.

Respect differences and similarities among the different breeds and different humans.

A person's a person no matter how small.

Stand up for yourself.

Always dream great dreams.

You are never too old to learn new things.

Don't be shy.

You are happiest when you help others.

It is good to be responsible for others.

Once you are responsible for someone, you must always help them.

Help whoever is truly good.

Help your brothers and sisters grow in selflessness.

Help those who are lonely and away from home.

Honor your teachers.

Know that art and beauty teach us lessons.

As I end my life, I go to my destiny knowing that I am well loved. I will soon climb those stairs to heaven, which will be hard for me since pugs are small and stairs are big. My grave goods will serve to teach the lessons of pug wisdom to those left behind. It is an honor to have lived with my family. It is an honor to have lived the life that my ancestor, General Celestial Wisdom, would have wanted me to live, and I will be greeted by him at the top of the stairs.

I am part of the Sheffield line of pugs bred by the divine pug breeder, Marjorie Shriver. We are the descendants of General Celestial Wisdom. Milton and Gracie, Shriver pugs, will take care of my family when I am gone. When they are gone, the responsibility for my family will go to another Shriver pug, Marcus Aurelius Pugmus Maximus, emperor of Rome and ruler of the known world. Hail Marcus.

I am not worried. General Celestial Wisdom and his descendants live in all pugs. Humans never fear when pugs are near.

Pugs. We must love mankind even though they are a lesser species—always anxious, always in a hurry. We pugs can accomplish great things with a flick of a paw or a lick on the cheek of an anxious human. It is our gift, for is not the pug a son of Buddha? We are one with the universe, and our souls float in the tranquility of the divine—
ommm-ommmm.

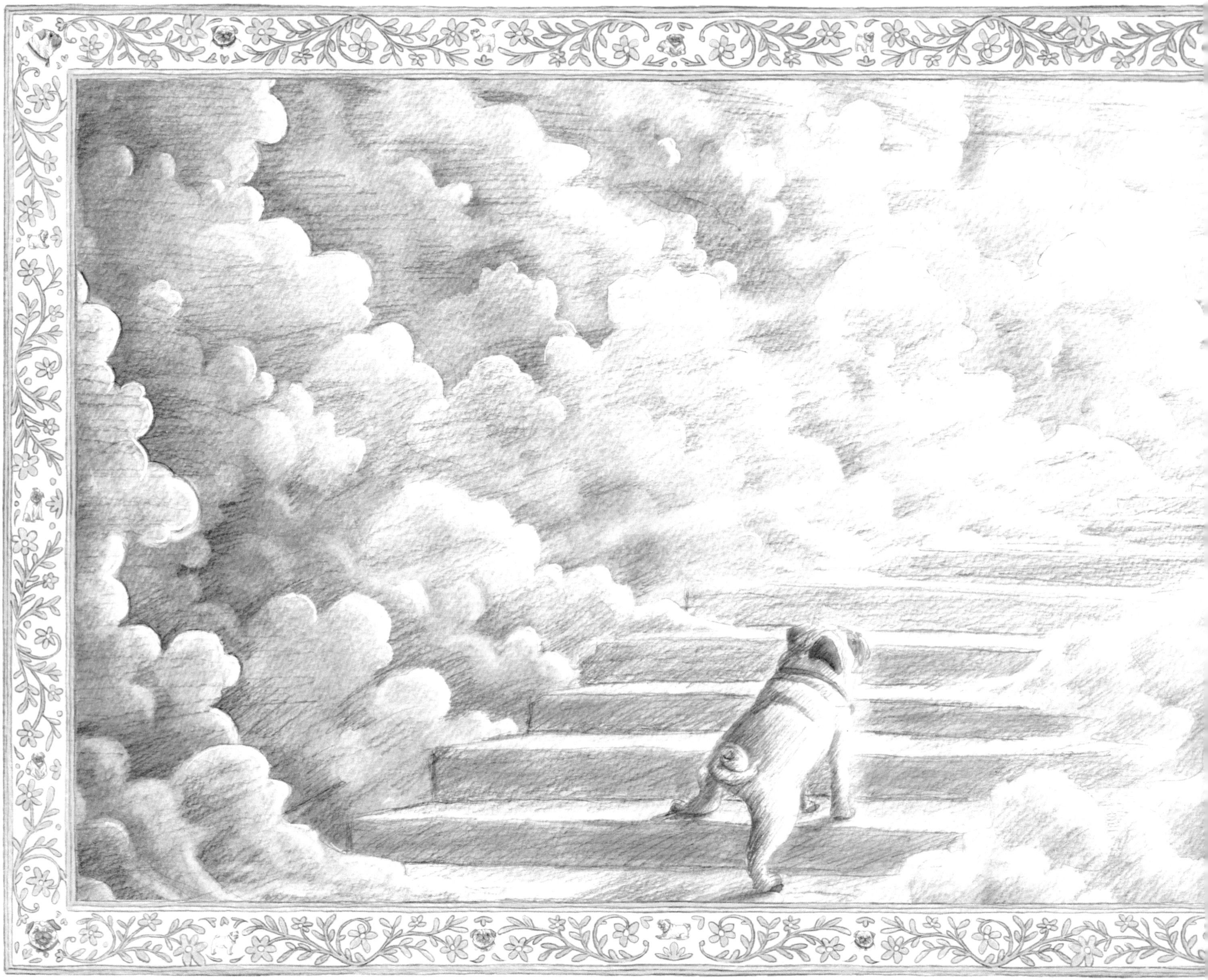

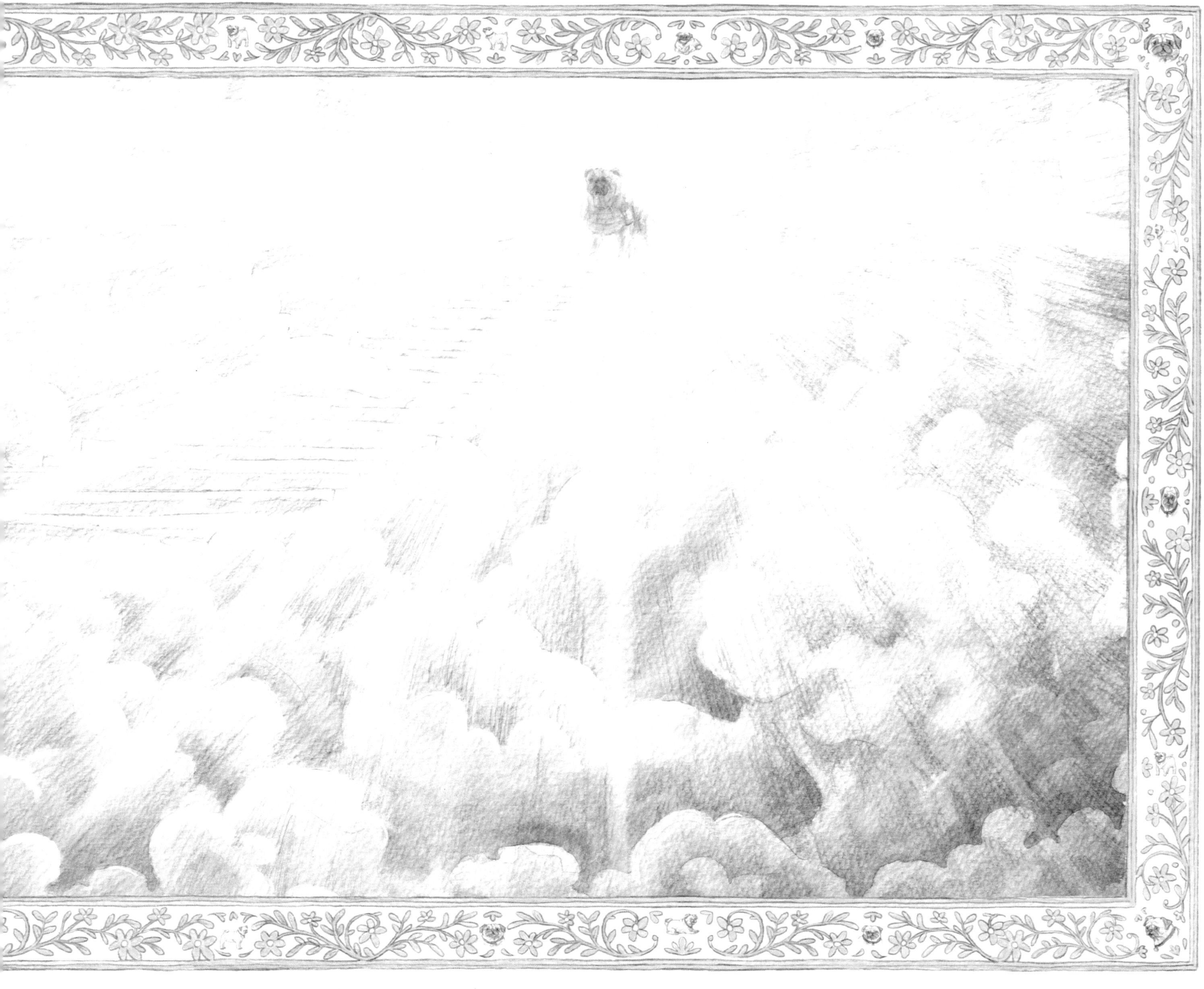

CPSIA information can be obtained
at www.ICGtesting.com
Printed in the USA
LVRC090123151221
706262LV00003B/48

* 9 7 8 1 6 4 6 6 3 6 2 2 8 *